Trail and Trading Post

Or, The Young Hunters of the Ohio

Edward Stratemeyer

Alpha Editions

This edition published in 2024

ISBN : 9789357965347

Design and Setting By
Alpha Editions
www.alphaedis.com
Email - info@alphaedis.com

Contents

PREFACE

"Trail and Trading Post" is a complete story in itself, but forms the sixth and last volume of a line known under the general title of "Colonial Series."

As I have mentioned before, when I started this series I had in mind to write not more than three volumes, telling of colonial times during the war between France and England for the possession of Canada and the territory bordering the Great Lakes. The first book, entitled "With Washington in the West," told of the disastrous Braddock campaign against Fort Duquesne; the second, called "Marching on Niagara," gave many of the particulars of General Forbes's advance against the same French stronghold and likewise the particulars of the advance of Generals Prideaux and Johnson against Fort Niagara; while the third volume, "At the Fall of Montreal," told of the heroic fighting of General Wolfe at Quebec, and that last contest which brought this long-drawn struggle to a close.

The war with France was now over, but the Indians were very bitter against the English, and in a fourth volume, called "On the Trail of Pontiac," were given the particulars of how that noted red warrior formed a conspiracy among a number of tribes to exterminate the English. The first conspiracy failed to come to a head, but Pontiac was not disheartened, and in a fifth volume, "The Fort in the Wilderness," were related how the warriors under him laid siege to Fort Detroit and Fort Pitt, and how the English under Colonel Bouquet won the bloody battle of Bushy Run,—the last regular contest with the red men for some years to come.

With the Indian struggle at an end, the English were more eager than ever to push forward to the west, to establish trading posts and settlements, and it is with this movement that the present volume concerns itself. The advance of the whites was watched with hatred by the Indians, who lost no opportunity to do them injury. Among those to push onward, to the fertile country bordering the Ohio River, were our old friends, the Morrises—and what they did to make our glorious country what it is to-day I leave the pages which follow to relate.

In closing this series I wish to thank the many thousands who have shown their appreciation of my efforts to amuse and instruct them. In penning the volumes I have endeavored to be as accurate historically as possible, and I trust the perusal will do my young readers much good.

EDWARD STRATEMEYER.

Independence Day, 1906.

CHAPTER I
A GLIMPSE OF THE PAST

"If we can only get that buffalo, Henry, it will be a feather in our cap."

"Right you are, Dave. But the animal may be miles and miles away by this time. As you know, they can run a long distance when they are frightened."

"Oh, yes, I know that well enough," answered Dave Morris, as he rested for a moment on the paddle he had been using. "I haven't forgotten the buffalo that once knocked our tent flat and ran away."

"And I haven't forgotten how I went after him and nearly lost my life tumbling over the rocks and down the big hill," added Henry. "I can tell you, I don't want another such experience!"

"Do you think the buffalo went around the head of the lake?"

"He was headed that way—the last I saw of him. Let us paddle up to the brook and go ashore. If the tracks are there we can follow them: if not, I reckon we'll have to give up the hunt and content ourselves with some small game."

"You don't suppose that there are any unfriendly Indians around," resumed Dave Morris, after a few minutes of silence, during which time both young hunters applied themselves to the paddles of the canoe they occupied. "I've had enough of fighting to last me for a long time to come."

"There is really no telling about that, the redskins are so treacherous. Down at the fort they seem to think the district for fifty miles around is clear, but Sam Barringford told me to keep my eyes peeled—that there is no telling yet what may happen. The war is over, but Pontiac isn't dead, and neither is Moon Eye, and a lot more of the other chiefs."

"Don't mention Moon Eye to me," said Dave Morris, with a shrug of his broad shoulders. "That Indian will never forgive me for escaping from him with Nell and the twins. I suppose he'd give a whole lot to get his hands on me again."

"As for that, he'd like to get his hands on any of the men who fought against him and his followers. The Indians think——Wait, Dave! Turn in to the shore, quick! I just saw the buffalo. He is back of the rocks over yonder!"

The canoe was turned in the direction indicated with all possible speed. Soon it glided under some overhanging bushes, and the paddles were stowed away noiselessly. Then each of the young hunters caught up his flint-lock musket, looked to the priming, to make certain that the weapon was ready for use, and stepped ashore.

"As you saw him first, you lead," whispered Dave Morris to his companion, and Henry led off, with the other youth close at his heels. Both had their eyes and ears on the alert for whatever might turn up.

As the old readers of this "Colonial Series" know, Dave and Henry Morris were cousins, of about the same age, who when at home lived near Will's Creek, Virginia—close to where the town of Cumberland now stands. Dave was the only son of a widower, James Morris, who was a well-known trapper and fur trader. Henry came of a more numerous family, he having an older brother Rodney and also a sister Nell, a bright miss of tender years.

In the first three volumes of this series, entitled, respectively, "With Washington in the West," "Marching on Niagara," and "At the Fall of Montreal," I told how Dave worked for the first President of our country when the latter was but a humble surveyor, and how the youth also served under his former employer during the memorable and disastrous Braddock advance on Fort Duquesne—held at that time, 1755, by the French, and located where the prosperous city of Pittsburg stands to-day. This was really the opening of the fourth intercolonial war, and was followed by an attack on Fort Niagara, and then by assaults on Quebec, Montreal, and other points, in which fights both Dave and Henry took active parts, doing their duty as common soldiers to the best of their ability.

With the close of the war between England and France, both of the young soldiers were glad enough to return home, which they did in company with a number of others, including Sam Barringford, a frontiersman who had been their friend through thick and thin, and also White Buffalo, an old chief of the Delawares, who was very friendly with all of the Morrises and who had done them more than one service.

Previous to the war Dave's father had established a small trading post in what was then considered the "far western country." This was on the Kinotah, a small but beautiful stream flowing into the Ohio River. The trader had a good deal of trouble with a rascally Frenchman, who claimed the post as his own, and who hired a number of Indians to make war on Mr. Morris, and at last the post had to be abandoned.

"I shall go and re-establish myself in the west," said James Morris, to his son and to his other relatives, and soon he set forth with a pack-train, as related in the fourth volume of this series, called "On the Trail of Pontiac." Dave and Henry went with him, and after a number of more or less thrilling adventures, the site of the post was reached. The place had been burned down, and the forest for a long distance around was a mass of blackened tree-stumps. Seeing this, the party journeyed further, presently reaching the Ohio, where a new post was established and held, despite the warlike attitude of Pontiac and many other Indian chiefs. Once the trader and his men had to retreat to Fort Pitt (formerly Fort Duquesne) for protection. A fierce fight was had with the enemy under Jean Bevoir, the rascally French trader who had caused the Morrises so much trouble, and nearly all of the enemy were killed, Bevoir himself being wounded both in the arm and the side.

Pontiac's first conspiracy against the English had come to naught, but the wily Indian leader was not dismayed, and soon he plotted to fall upon many of the settlements simultaneously. What this led to has been related in detail in the fifth volume of this series, entitled "The Fort in the Wilderness," Fort Detroit was besieged and likewise Fort Pitt and many other points of lesser importance, and had it not been for the advance of an English army from the east, with victories at Bushy Run and other points, there is no doubt but that the massacre of the settlers would have been appalling. As it was, James Morris had to abandon his new trading post, and he and Henry, with some others, reached Fort Pitt only after a desperate struggle to escape the red men.

Dave, during this trouble, was at the home near Will's Creek. Here the effects of the uprising were also felt. White Buffalo, the ever-faithful friend, brought word to the Morrises, and they took their flight to Fort Cumberland just in the nick of time.

During a previous winter, when the snow lay deep upon the ground, the old frontiersman, Sam Barringford, had made a curious discovery. Wrapped in a bundle swinging from a tree he had found two boy babies, evidently twins. He had carried the twins to the Morris cabin, where Mrs. Morris had taken care of the babes, who, later on, were named Tom and Artie. Barringford learned through White Buffalo that a Frenchman at Detroit knew something about the twins and he determined to visit the fort, taking Dave with him. The trip brought to light little that was new, but the old frontiersman and the young soldier saw how Fort Detroit was besieged and had much trouble in getting away. Then, in company with Rodney Morris, the two joined the English army marching westward to relieve Fort Pitt. After the battle of Bushy Run Dave was made a prisoner by some Indians under Moon Eye and taken to a village, where, to his surprise, he also found the twins and Nell, they having been stolen some time previous. Watching his chances, the young soldier managed to escape in a canoe during a violent storm, taking the little twins and his cousin with him. Later he was aided by White Buffalo, and though the Indians under Moon Eye did their best to retake their captives, they were soon halted by James Morris, Rodney, Barringford, Henry, and some of the English regulars, and were forced to leave that section of the country. Dave continued on his way to Fort Pitt with his relatives and friends; and there the whole party rested for the time being. In the meantime word was received from the east that matters had quieted down around Will's Creek, so that Joseph Morris and his wife could return to the old homestead, for which those at the fort were thankful.

"I'd like to be back home myself," said Rodney. In years gone by he had been almost a cripple and the campaign against the Indians had told greatly upon him.

"I think you had better start before long," his uncle had answered. "Your father will need you, and besides Nell and the twins must get back."

While at Fort Pitt the Morrises and Sam Barringford had come in contact with Benoit Vascal, the Frenchman who knew something about the twins. They thought Vascal had stolen the children from their parents, but the Frenchman laid the blame on one Paul Camont, who had been killed by the wolves at the spot where Tom and Artie were found. Benoit Vascal said the children belonged to a Mr. Maurice Hamilton, a gentleman who had visited America to look up some land claims. It was said that Mr. Hamilton had returned to London almost a year before. A letter was sent to England, but in those days it took a long time to cross the ocean, and so far no answer had been received. It had been decided to keep Benoit Vascal a prisoner at Fort Pitt, but the wily Frenchman slipped away and left for parts unknown.

CHAPTER II
A BUFFALO AND A BEAR

Two weeks had passed quietly at Fort Pitt when Dave suggested to Henry that they go out on a hunt for large game. In the meantime it was arranged that Rodney, Sam Barringford, and a number of others should journey to the east, taking little Nell and the twins with them. The start was to be made on the following Monday, and this was Thursday.

"You must be very careful," said Mr. Morris, when the two young hunters set out on their quest for big game. "Run no needless chances, and if you see any unfriendly Indians lose no time in returning to this fort."

It was the middle of September—a clear, cool day, with a faint breeze blowing from the northward. Dave and Henry had set out directly after breakfast, each armed with his long flint-lock musket and his day's rations. Both wore their old army uniforms, which were much the worse for the hard usage received. But, as Dave remarked, anything was good enough for the forest, where nobody was likely to see them.

Three hours of tramping had brought them to a small body of water, called by the Indians Lake Kashaka. Here, drifting about, they came across an Indian canoe containing two good paddles. Without hesitation they entered the canoe and crossed the lake, where they came upon the track of several deer. They were deliberating upon whether to follow the trail or not when Henry chanced to look up the lake and see a buffalo near some rocks. The animal was gazing at them with lifted head, and almost instantly ran from sight behind some bushes.

"There's our meat!" cried Henry, and dashed back to the canoe. Then he told of what he had seen, and the boys made after the game, as already described. Buffaloes were not so plentiful in this section of the country as they had been previous to the coming of the English and French hunters, and the idea of bringing down so much good meat at a single shooting filled the youths with keen enthusiasm.

It took the two young hunters but a few minutes to reach the spot where Henry had seen the buffalo. The game was not in sight, but the marks of his hoofs were plainly to be seen and some young and tender bushes showed where he had been browsing.

"'Tis only a question of how far he had traveled," said Henry, who had always been considered the best hunter among the Morris boys. "It may be only a quarter of a mile, and then again it may be six or eight miles."

"Let us follow the trail, at least for awhile," answered Dave. "It is plain enough. He must be a pretty heavy fellow, by the depth of the marks he has left."

"I imagine all full-grown buffaloes are rather heavy," answered Henry. "Come on, and do not make any more noise than is necessary. We don't want him to get scared again—if he is within hearing."

The trail of the buffalo led up a small hill and then down into a bit of meadow, where the grass was thick and damp. As the youths progressed a flock of birds started up directly in front of them and presently they caught sight of three fair-sized rabbits.

"Now just look at that!" cried Dave, in vexed tones. "They seem to know that we are afraid to shoot at them, for fear of disturbing the bigger game."

"Puts me in mind of what Ira Sanderson once said," returned his cousin with a grin. "He argued that a fellow always saw the best game when he was out without his shooting-iron."

"I reckon he was right, Henry; I've seen some fine deer when I didn't have anything to shoot with."

The two young hunters now relapsed into silence, as the meadow came to an end and they entered the forest. Here there was a buffalo trail well defined, having been used by the animals for many years. The trail in general was old, but the fresh hoofmarks of the single animal that had just passed were easily followed by Henry, who was as good on a trail as the average Indian.

The forest was a primeval one, with great trees stretching their branches in all directions. Monstrous roots lay sprawled over the trail, and they had to watch out that one or the other did not take a tumble. The air was filled with the songs and cries of birds, while here and there they heard the steady tap-tap of the woodpecker at his work. They could have brought down a dozen squirrels had they felt so inclined, and not a few chipmunks also showed themselves.

"That buffalo must have gone quite a way," remarked Henry, as they came to a halt in the midst of a forest glade. "We have already covered a good mile and a half."

"Don't give up yet," pleaded Dave, who had set his heart on returning to Fort Pitt with the news of laying low the bison.

"Oh, I'm willing enough to go on, Dave. But we have got to leave the regular trail now."

"Where is the new trail?"

"Over yonder," and Henry pointed with his hand.

"It seems to me he left the regular trail rather suddenly," remarked Dave, walking over to the spot indicated. "Don't you think so?"

"I do."

"What for?"

"I don't know, excepting that something must have scared him—some rabbits in the brush, or something like that."

Once more the two young hunters pushed forward, the trail now leading among some rocks, where walking was anything but agreeable. In some places there were sharp brambles which scratched them not a little.

"Henry, that buffalo didn't come this way for nothing," whispered Dave.

"Just what I think. He was scared, and scared good and proper too. I wish I knew what did it."

"Can there be any other hunters around here?"

"That isn't impossible. A number of the men who were at the fort have gone away in the last few days. Some of them may be in this vicinity."

"If they are I trust we shoot that buffalo first."

They now reached another rise of ground, beyond which was a depression encircled by bushes and rocks. As they mounted the rise they heard a peculiar snort.

"Listen!" whispered Henry, and held up his hand.

"It's the buffalo!" answered his cousin. "And hark! Some other animal is there!"

"I think I know what it is, Dave. Be careful now and don't make any more noise."

Guns to the front, they crawled up the rise and peered through the fringe of brushwood. A sight met their gaze that thrilled them to the heart.

The buffalo was there, heavy-set and shaggy as to head and shoulders, and with a look of fierceness in his staring eyes. He was crouched beside a rock, and directly in front of him was a small she-bear, standing on her hind legs, and with her jaws dripping with blood. Behind the bear were two half-grown cubs, both whining because of wounds in their sides.

To Henry's practiced eye the scene told its own story. In leaping over the rise of ground the buffalo had come close to the den of the bear and had stepped on both of the cubs, who were probably playing around at the time. This had aroused the ire of the mother bear, and she had sprung to the rescue and bitten the buffalo in the flank. The big beast, unable to proceed on his flight, had turned around and struck the bear in the side. Then both had separated, and were now getting ready to renew the contest between them.

Both had separated, and were now getting ready to renew the contest.

The mother bear now uttered a peculiar sound, and at this the cubs retreated to a hole under some rocks, which was their home. The next instant the buffalo charged once more, hitting the bear squarely on the head and knocking her over. But as she tumbled, she caught her enemy by the neck and sank her teeth deeply into the buffalo's throat.

"What a fight!" whispered Dave. "What shall we do?"

"Wait—but be ready to shoot," answered Henry. "I think the buffalo will try to run for it in another minute."

There was a snarl and a snort, and the buffalo did his best to throw the bear off. But the latter clung fast, in the meantime clawing rapidly with her hind feet at the bison's forequarter. Then the buffalo swung around, knocking the smaller beast against the rocks with such force that the two young hunters heard the ribs of the bear crack. She fell to the ground and the buffalo struck at her repeatedly with his hoofs.

"It's all over with the bear," whispered Dave. "Hadn't we better shoot at the buffalo?"

Before Henry could reply, the bison swung around once more and made a leap which, for the instant, took him out of sight of both youths. His instinct told him of more danger in that vicinity, and he sprang up on some rocks to get a better look around. This movement brought him face to face with Dave and Henry.

Crack! It was the report of Henry's gun, and the bullet hit the bison on the side of the head, not far from the left eye. But the shot was merely a glancing one and did little damage. Then Dave fired, hitting the beast in the fleshy part of the neck.

The fight with the bear had left the buffalo in anything but a good humor and the two shots from the young hunters only added to his ugliness. He paused to glare at the pair and then made a savage leap towards Henry, lowering his horns as he did so.

"Look out!" screamed Dave, and Henry sprang to one side. The movement was so quick that he could not calculate on where he was going and he slipped into a hollow, his right foot going down between two heavy stones in such a fashion that his ankle was badly wrenched.

The buffalo now turned upon Dave and he too leaped away. With unloaded gun he could do nothing, and as quickly as possible he started to put in a fresh charge and fix the priming. In the meantime the buffalo swung around once more, gave Henry and the bear another look, and then sprang for the brushwood and was out of sight in a twinkling.

CHAPTER III
DAVE AND THE INDIAN

"He has gone!"

"Shoot him, Dave, shoot him!"

With frantic haste Dave fixed the priming of his flint-lock musket. But long before the weapon was ready for use the buffalo was out of sight and hearing.

On the ground in the hollow lay the she-bear, giving a last convulsive shudder. At the mouth of her den were the two cubs, whining plaintively, as if they understood that something had gone wrong. Henry sat on one of the rocks, with his foot still caught fast and a look of pain on his face.

"What's the matter? Did the buffalo hit you?" called out his cousin, after he had looked to make certain that the bear could do no further harm.

"No, but I—I hurt my ankle," panted Henry. He gave his leg a pull. "Oh! But that hurts!"

"The bear is out of it," said Dave. He came closer. "Hullo, your foot is caught. Let me help you. I reckon we have seen the last of that buffalo."

"I don't know about that, Dave. We both hit him, and the bear gave him something to remember her by."

"Poor beast! She certainly did what she could for her cubs. Just look at them now!"

It was an affecting sight. The mother bear had passed away and both of the cubs had crawled forth from the den and were licking her face and pushing her form with their little noses. Then both began to whine once more. Neither seemed to think of running away.

Dave set down his gun and helped Henry to release his caught foot. Then they took off the legging and the shoe. The ankle had begun to swell and there was a deep scratch on one side.

"Can you step on it?" asked Dave, and his cousin tried to do so. He caught his breath and gave a gasp.

"Like pins and needles going through my leg!" he announced. "Oh, what luck! And we didn't get the buffalo after all!" he added, ruefully.

The bear cubs now came up and one made a snap at Dave's foot while the other took up Henry's shoe and began to chew it. Seeing this, Dave drew his hunting knife and dispatched them both. Then he turned again to his cousin.

"I suppose it is out of the question for you to think of walking," he said.

"Not just yet," answered Henry. "Maybe I'll be able to do it in an hour or two."

"Then we may as well rest right here. One comfort, we have the bear and her cubs even if we didn't get the buffalo."

"Dave, why don't you follow the trail again? That buffalo may not be far off. It won't do any good for you to sit down here by me—I can take care of myself. Only be careful that the beast doesn't corner you."

"I'll do it. But I'll get you some water first," answered Dave.

He had noted a spring just before coming to the bear hollow, and he walked back to it and procured some water in a gourd they carried for that purpose. With this Henry started to bathe his swollen ankle, while Dave took to the fresh trail the buffalo had made.

"Don't stay away more than an hour!" called out Henry after him.

"Not unless it takes a little longer to get a good chance at the buffalo," replied his cousin.

The buffalo had crashed through a long stretch of brushwood where the trail could be followed with ease. Then he had taken to the old trail once more, at a point a good half-mile from where he had before left it.

"He is bound for the west, that's certain," said Dave to himself. "And more than likely he will keep on until sundown. I may as well give up all hopes of bringing him down. Heigh-ho! such are the fortunes of hunting!" And he heaved a deep sigh.

He kept on for quarter of a mile further, reaching a point where the trail crossed a small but clear stream of spring water. Here the bison had paused for a drink, and resting his gun against a tree, the young hunter got down on his hands and knees to do likewise.

The water tasted so good that Dave took his time and drank his fill. Then he raised his head, started to rise, and looked toward the tree where he had placed his weapon.

The gun was gone!

For the moment the young hunter could not believe the evidence of his senses. He remained in a crouching position, wondering what he had best do. He felt that an enemy must have taken the gun, and wondered who it could be. With caution he looked around, but not a soul was in sight.

It was a peculiar position to be in, and small wonder that the cold perspiration stood out upon the young hunter's forehead. He had been in peril before, among the Indians, and felt fairly certain that a red man had gotten the better of him.

What was best to do? He asked himself the question several times, his heart beating meanwhile like a trip-hammer within his breast. An enemy was surely at hand. What would be the next movement of the unknown?

Cautiously he put his hand to his side, drew his hunting knife, and arose slowly to an upright position. Overhead the branches of the trees were tightly interlaced, making the spot rather gloomy. The stream came down between a number of rocks which were backed up by bushes and trees. Would it be best to make a dash for this shelter?

"White boy drop knife!"

The unexpected command, issued in a guttural tone, came from a clump of brushwood behind Dave. The young hunter swung around, but could see no one.

"White boy drop knife, or Indian shoot," were the next words spoken, and now Dave saw the barrel of his own gun pointed at his breast.

"Who are you?" he asked.

"White boy drop knife, or shoot him sure!" was the only answer, and now the muzzle of the gun was shoved a little closer to the youth's breast. Looking through the brushwood, Dave made out the repulsive features of a savage and saw the wicked gleam of his black eyes.

There seemed to be no help for it, and the hunting knife dropped to the ground. The Indian gave a grunt of satisfaction and then stepped into the opening, still, however, keeping the gun levelled at Dave's breast. He was a brawny warrior of the Senecas, arrayed in his war-paint and feathers, and he carried a tomahawk and a knife in his girdle and a bow with arrows across his shoulders.

"Where white boy come from?" he asked, abruptly.

"I came from Fort Pitt," answered Dave. "Why did you steal my gun?"

At the last question the red man gave a grunt that might mean anything. He looked Dave over with care and made him back away, so that he could secure the lad's hunting knife, which he placed beside his own.

"White boy sodger, um?" went on the savage, noting the tattered uniform.

"Yes, I have been a soldier," answered Dave. He continued to gaze at the savage. "I've seen you before. Oh, I remember now. You were with Moon Eye, right after I was captured. You had something to do with the stealing of my little cousin and the twin boys."

- 13 -

The red man's eyes flashed, but he did not answer to this. Evidently he was pondering upon what to do next. He had come upon Dave quite unexpectedly and had taken the gun on the impulse of the moment.

"White boy alone?" he asked, after an awkward pause.

"No, I have a good many friends around here," was Dave's quick reply, but he did not add that the majority of his friends were at the fort.

At this the face of the warrior darkened. He allowed the gun barrel to drop and drew his tomahawk. If others of the whites were near he thought it might be best to brain Dave on the spot, making as little noise as possible, and then get away from that vicinity.

The young hunter understood the movement, and his heart leaped into his throat. He had no desire to feel the edge of the savage's stone hatchet. As the gun barrel dropped still lower he thought of the rocks and the brushwood and made a spring towards them.

"*Pawah!*" cried the Indian, in a rage. "White boy stop!" And he made a dash after the youth. But as luck would have it one moccasin caught in a trailing vine and he pitched headlong. As he went down, the trigger of the gun struck some brush, caught fast, and the piece went off with a loud report.

Dave imagined the gun was discharged at himself, and fully expected to feel the sting of the bullet, perhaps in some vital portion of his body. He felt himself making a silent prayer, and as the sting did not come realized that as yet he was unharmed. He cleared the rocks at another bound, almost fell into the bushes, and ran on and on with all the speed he could command.

Dave covered a good quarter of a mile before he thought of coming to a halt. He was now in the very depths of the great forest, with a heavy growth of timber on all sides of him. The way had been rough and he had stumbled twice, scratching his hand and his knee so that they smarted greatly. He was far away from the buffalo trail and also away from the stream where he had stopped for a drink. He had made a number of turns while running, and could not tell in what direction he had left either the red warrior or Henry.

"Here's a fine kettle of fish!" he muttered, as he stopped to catch his breath. "Everything is going wrong to-day. First we lost the buffalo, then Henry sprained his ankle, and now here am I, trying to get away from a redskin who wants to take my life and who has robbed me of my rifle and hunting knife! I wonder what will happen next?"

He listened intently, but could hear nothing of his red foe, nor could he see anything to alarm him. It was more gloomy than ever under the trees, the sun having gone under a cloud. The breeze sighed mournfully through the tallest branches, and only the occasional note of a bird, or the distant bark of a fox, broke the stillness.

Dave did not dare to linger long in one spot, fearing that the Indian might be sneaking over his trail with the slyness of a fox. He pushed forward, hoping to come to a series of rocks, or a deep stream, where the trail might be hidden.

His search was at last rewarded. Some flat rocks appeared, forming something of a cliff. He walked over these, taking care to avoid every accumulation of dirt or trailing vines. Then, coming to the end of the stones, he leaped down into a gully, where flowed a stream of water several feet wide and more than a foot deep. He followed this stream a long distance, until it was lost among some rugged rocks, where his further progress appeared to be barred.

"There—I don't think that Indian can follow me to here," he told himself. "The question is, How am I to get back to Henry without being discovered, and how are we both to get back to the fort?"

CHAPTER IV
TAKEN BY SURPRISE

Dave's hasty flight had tired him out, and he was glad enough to sit down upon one of the rocks and rest. The cloudiness in the sky had continued, and it looked as if there might be a shower before nightfall.

The young hunter was in anything but a cheerful frame of mind, and would have given a good deal to have been back at the fort once more. He was worried also about his cousin, and trusted that Henry would not fall into the hands of the Indian.

At last, having gotten back his breath, he resolved to start off once more and see if he could not locate the spot where he had left his cousin. He walked through the forest with extreme caution, often coming to a halt, to survey the surroundings and make sure that the enemy was nowhere near.

Thus a full hour more was consumed, and he knew that Henry would now be growing exceedingly anxious concerning his prolonged absence.

"I hope he doesn't try to follow me up," said Dave to himself. "If he does it's more than likely that redskin will see him."

At length, after moving in several directions, the young hunter came to a spot that looked slightly familiar to him. He made a circle of the point, and finally recognized it as the very spot he had come to with White Buffalo when he and the Indian were on the way to the fort with little Nell and the twins.

"Well, I never thought I'd see this place again!" he murmured, half aloud. "I wish I had White Buffalo with me now. I'd feel a heap safer than I do."

He now knew how to reach the fort, and resolved to follow that course until he should come to the point where the trail crossed that which he and Henry had taken after leaving the lake to go after the buffalo. Then he would follow up the buffalo trail to where his cousin had been left.

He tramped on and on, growing bolder as he saw nothing more of his red enemy. It was well past noon, and he munched some of the rations in his game bag, washing down the hasty meal with more water from a brook.

He was almost up to the spot where the fight between the buffalo and the bear had occurred when he suddenly heard the murmur of voices, conversing in the Indian language. Looking to one side of the clearing, he made out four Indians, one of whom was the fellow who had deprived him of his rifle and hunting knife.

The discovery came as a shock to Dave, and once again his heart sank within him. He had presence of mind enough to leap behind some bushes, and a moment later the red men passed within three yards of him. Then he heard a cry from the Indians, followed by an exclamation from Henry.

"They have found him!" thought Dave, and he was right. The four red men came upon poor Henry just as he was putting on his shoe, preparatory to looking for his cousin. One leaped forward, pinning the young hunter to the rocks, and in a twinkling the four had made him a prisoner and disarmed him.

"What does this mean?" demanded Henry, although he knew only too well. "Let up, I say!" But the Indians paid no attention. One carried a length of rawhide and with this they bound the young hunter's hands behind him. Then his pockets were searched, and they took from him the three shillings and sixpence he happened to be carrying.

After the capture, the four Indians held a consultation among themselves. It was in their native tongue, so that Henry could understand next to nothing.

"White boy come with Indians," said the red man who could speak English. He had joined his brother warriors after giving up the chase after Dave.

At that moment Henry caught sight of the extra hunting knife and the rifle he knew only too well.

"Dave's gun and Dave's knife!" he cried. "What have you done with him?" he asked, with a sinking heart.

The Indian would not answer this question, but drew up his eyes in a peculiar fashion that caused Henry to shiver. He concluded that Dave must have been killed, although he noted with just a grain of hope that none of the warriors carried his cousin's scalp.

Despite the fact that his ankle hurt him a good deal, Henry was forced to march along with the Indians, who prodded him now and then with the points of their hunting knives to make him move along faster. The course was to the northwest, to a stream known to the red men as the Mustalonack, where a small band had taken up their secret abode since the disastrous battle of Bushy Run.

After what was to Henry a painful walk lasting an hour, the Mustalonack was reached, and from the bushes along the bank the Indians drew a long canoe. They made Henry enter and then got in themselves and shoved off. The course was up the stream, and two used the paddles. As the current was rather swift, the progress of the craft was necessarily slow.

In moving towards the river the Indians had been on the alert for the possible appearance of white hunters or English soldiers. They knew that to stay in that neighborhood was dangerous, and they expected in a few days to move much further to the westward, perhaps even as far as the Mississippi. They were awaiting orders from their chief, who, in turn, was hoping every day to receive some wampum, or speech belt, from Pontiac.

But though the red warriors were on the alert, their eyes were not sharp enough to catch sight of Dave, as he followed them at a safe distance. Although unarmed, the young hunter could not bear to think of leaving his cousin to his fate, and so he kept the party in front in sight, hoping that sooner or later he would be able to render Henry some assistance.

When the Indians set off in the canoe, Dave was for the moment nonplussed, not knowing how to follow them. But when he saw how slowly the craft moved, he took courage, and walking through the forest along the shore, managed, although not without an effort, to keep them in sight until they had journeyed as far as they wished, when he saw them land on the opposite shore, pull the long canoe into the bushes, and hurry once more into the forest.

To some faint-hearted persons this might have meant the end of the pursuit, but Dave was made of sterner stuff, and besides he loved his cousin too dearly to give up the hope of a rescue thus readily. He saw that the stream at this point was rather shallow, and without hesitation pulled off his shoes and stockings, rolled up his breeches, and waded in.

Fording the stream was not as easy as it looked, and more than once Dave was in danger of slipping down on the loose rocks or of having the current carry him off his feet. But he managed to reach the opposite shore of the stream in safety, and there, donning his stockings and shoes again, hurried on after the red men as before.

Dave had not gone very far when he saw the unmistakable signs of an Indian village. He slackened his pace and soon saw a lean and hungry-looking Indian dog coming toward him. The canine began to bark viciously and showed his teeth.

Here it was that the young hunter's nerve again showed itself. He was well acquainted with the general worthlessness of the Indian curs—dogs that were not to be compared with the hunting and watch animals of the English— and picking up a sharp stone he let drive, taking the canine in the side. The dog gave a sharp yelp, turned and fled, and that was the last Dave saw of the animal.

In the meantime the Indians had arrived at their temporary village, located in a dense portion of the forest, and consisting of nothing more than half a dozen dirty shelters of blankets and skins. In the center was a small clearing where a campfire smoldered, and around this lolled half a dozen Indians, while not far off were several squaws and a dozen dirty and half-clad Indian children.

The coming of the four warriors with their captive produced a mild sensation, and there was a running fire of questions and answers in the native dialect, lasting some time. In the meanwhile two of the warriors bound Henry to a tree near the largest of the wigwams, and left him, for the time being, to take care of himself.

The head of the tribe, Moon Eye, was away, and was not expected back until the next day at noon. This being so, the Indians decided to keep Henry where he was. He was given nothing to eat, and when he asked for a drink he was handed some dirty water that even a dog would have refused.

"What do you want of me?" Henry asked, of the Indian who could speak English.

"White boy wait and he shall see," answered the warrior.

"Did you kill my cousin—the one who owns that rifle and the hunting knife?"

"White boy must not ask so many questions."

"If you don't let me go you'll get into trouble," went on Henry, thinking he might scare the Indians into releasing him. "See how you have already suffered. The English have many soldiers—they can do the red men great harm."

"The French have many soldiers also," answered the warrior. "Soon their army will come to the aid of Pontiac and his followers."

This was a story that had often been told to the red men by the French traders, and many of the Indians believed it. But they waited in vain for help from France, or from Canada. Instead of sending help, the king of France sold his holding along the Mississippi to Spain, so that the Indians were worse off than ever.

As night came on it began to rain gently, while a heavy mist filled the air. The Indians did not like this at all, and after huddling around the campfire for awhile the majority of them crawled into the wigwams and went to sleep. Two of them visited Henry, binding him more securely to the tree than ever, so that to break or slip his bonds was entirely out of the question.

"White boy sleep good," said one of them, as a joke, and then both stalked over to the fire once more. But the rain and the mist were not to their liking and presently they, too, retired. Then the fire died down gradually, and the Indian village became as quiet as a graveyard.

CHAPTER V
THE FLIGHT TO THE RIVER

"Henry!"

"Dave! How did you manage——"

"Hush! Don't make any noise, or the Indians may hear you. Stand still until I untie the ropes. They took my knife away from me."

No more was said just then. Henry's heart gave a great bound of joy. Dave was alive and well, after all. The discovery was almost too good to be true.

With dextrous fingers Dave undid the rawhide which held his cousin a prisoner. Henry was so stiff that he staggered, and Dave had to support him for the moment.

"Come with me to the river—we can take to the canoe," whispered Dave into his cousin's ear. He was fearful that one of the Indians might awaken at any moment and stop their flight.

"All right, Dave, but——" Henry hesitated, and tried to look through the darkness and the rain. "Are you armed?"

"No."

"Neither am I—they took everything I had. We ought to try to get at least one rifle and a knife."

"Yes, but the risk?"

"Is the canoe ready for use?"

"Yes,—all we have to do is to jump in and shove off."

"Then keep still until I take a look around. At the first sign of an alarm make for the canoe as tight as you can."

Henry's wrenched ankle still pained him, but in the excitement of the occasion he paid no attention to the injury. With the wiliness of the red warriors he was trying to outwit, he crawled forward in the darkness until he was close to one of the wigwams. This he knew held several Indians and also his own weapons and those belonging to Dave.

With bated breath the young hunter raised the dirty flap to the wigwam and tried to pierce the darkness inside. He could see next to nothing. He crawled in a little further, and his hand came in contact with an Indian's foot. He felt further, and touched the barrel of a gun. He raised the weapon and drew it towards him. One of the red men gave a deep sigh and a grunt, but did not awaken.

Encouraged by his success so far, Henry crawled forward again and this time obtained the second rifle, the powder horns, and also one of the hunting knives. His eyes were now becoming accustomed to the darkness, and finding a tomahawk he took that too, and then a bow and a quiver full of arrows.

At that instant one of the Indians turned over, muttering in his sleep. Fearful that he was awakening, the young hunter made a hasty move toward the wigwam opening. He stepped on the foot of a sleeping warrior, and the red man sat up with a start and called out in his native tongue, demanding to know what was the matter. Then, as he saw Henry dart from the shelter, he gave a war-cry that alarmed the entire camp.

"Lead the way to the canoe, Dave!" cried Henry. "And here, take one of these rifles. If they press us too closely, fire!"

Dave took the weapon handed to him, and side by side they rushed toward the river. Hardly had they gained the shelter of the forest when the red warriors were in full pursuit. One caught up a dying brand from the fire, and swinging it in a circle soon had it burning brightly for a torch.

Fortunately for the two young hunters, Dave had noted the trail to the river with care, so that he did not get mixed up, even though it was dark and misty. But Henry could not run very fast on account of his lame ankle.

"I'm glad we are to—to go by way of the—the river," he gasped. "I—I can't run much further!"

The Indians were yelling wildly, and one of them let fly an arrow which whizzed through the bushes at their side. Dave caught his cousin by the arm, to aid him, and an instant later another arrow flew directly between their heads.

"They must see us, Henry. Come, can't you run just a bit faster?"

"I'll—I'll try," gasped Henry, and gritted his teeth, so great was the pain in his ankle.

The forest now came to an end, but luckily for the youths the river was bordered with thick brushwood. Into this they dove, and in half a minute more reached the point where Dave had left the canoe in readiness for immediate flight.

"It's gone!" cried the young hunter, in dismay.

"The canoe?" queried his cousin.

"Yes, I left it right here."

"Then we are lost!"

Sick at heart, they caught each other by the arm and listened. The Indians were close at hand. What was to be done?

"Let us try to trick them!" whispered Dave, and caught up a stone that was handy. He threw it into the water with a splash, and then threw another stone after it. This accomplished, he drew Henry into the bushes, and both made their way down the shore for a good hundred feet, walking in shallow water to conceal the trail.

The mist over the water was thicker than in the forest, and when the Indians came out on the shore they could see little or nothing, even though they swung the torch in all directions.

"They leaped into the water,—I heard them," said one warrior, in the Indian language.

"I heard them too," answered another. "They must be swimming for the other side."

"We'll get into the canoe and look around," put in a third.

They ran to where the long canoe had been left, and then uttered cries of anger at finding the craft missing.

"They have taken the canoe!"

"If that is so we cannot catch them—the mist will hide them from view."

"Moon Eye will be angry when he finds his best canoe gone," grumbled the Indian who could speak English. "And my bow is gone too!"

The Indians continued to walk up and down the river bank, looking for some trace of the two whites. They could not imagine who had come to Henry's rescue, but thought it must be somebody from Fort Pitt, and were much disturbed, thinking that some English soldiers might be in that vicinity.

Meanwhile Dave and Henry remained hidden in the bushes, close to the water's edge. They caught an occasional flash from the torch, but otherwise saw nothing of their enemies. The cooling water seemed to soothe Henry's ankle greatly, for which the young hunter was grateful.

"Let us go on a little further," whispered Henry, after a short rest, and while the Indians were out of sight and hearing. "The further we get away, the better."

Dave was more than willing, and they moved through the shallow water until they reached a bend in the river. Then both gave a cry of satisfaction:

"The canoe!"

"It must have drifted to this spot," said Dave. "See, the paddles are just as I left them. But I thought the canoe was fast."

"Get in and be quick about it," returned his cousin.

They entered the craft and shoved out into the stream. The rain had ceased, but the mist was so thick they could scarcely see two yards in any direction. Catching up the paddles, they guided the canoe down the watercourse as best they could. At first they caught a faint glimpse of the Indians' torch, but this was quickly swallowed up by the mist and darkness.

"I reckon we are out of it," said Dave, after quarter of an hour had passed. "And I am glad of it." He heaved a long sigh of relief.

"You are not half as glad as I am," answered his cousin. "I felt pretty blue when they had me tied to the tree, I can tell you! How ever did you locate me?"

"It's a long story," answered Dave, and then told of his meeting with the Indian who could speak English, and of what had happened afterward.

"We can certainly count ourselves more than lucky," said Henry. "In nine cases out of ten those redskins would have killed us on the spot, and scalped us in the bargain. They are terribly bitter because Pontiac's last conspiracy failed."

"I think I know why they let you live, Henry. They wanted to learn how matters stood at the fort. They'd make you tell everything, even if they had to torture you into doing it."

"I reckon you are right on that point."

Feeling themselves safe for the time being, the two young hunters stopped paddling and tried to gaze around them. Nothing could be seen but the mist and water, the latter rushing along with increased swiftness.

"Did they have another canoe?" asked Henry, presently.

"I couldn't find any, and I looked pretty carefully."

"In that case, they won't be able to follow us very readily."

"They won't know where to look for us, in this darkness, Henry. The question is, where are we going? I know nothing of this river, do you?"

"I do not, but I imagine it flows into the Allegheny or the Ohio."

"If it will take us to the fort, that is just where we want to go."

They talked the matter over, and decided to keep on the river at least for a few miles further. Then they would go ashore, make themselves as comfortable as possible, and wait for daylight to appear.

"If the sun comes out we can climb a tall tree and get the lay of the land," said Dave. "Or, I can climb it alone, since your ankle is hurt. How does it feel now?"

"No worse," answered his cousin. "I think if I can keep off it for a few hours it will be all right again. But it was a pretty bad twist."

"Do you notice that the river seems to be growing narrower?" said Dave, after a short spell of silence.

"I have been wondering if we are not on some branch," was the reply. "Anyway, it is flowing much swifter than before."

"Maybe we had better turn into shore now."

"I think so myself. We don't want to run into anything."

They started to turn the canoe around. To their surprise the water began to boil and foam on all sides of them. Then came a grating sound from the bottom.

"We just ran over a rock!" cried Dave. "Henry, this is getting dangerous!"

"I think so myself, Dave. Come, we will make for the shore over yonder. Perhaps—— Oh!"

Henry's remarks came to a sudden ending, as the canoe swept swiftly under the low-hanging branch of a big tree. The young hunter was standing up at the time, and he was carried overboard in a flash, paddle in hand. Then the canoe struck a rock, slid up along some tree-roots, and began to fill with water!

CHAPTER VI
BACK TO THE FORT

Henry was so taken by surprise that it was not until he found himself over his head in the river he realized what had occurred. His shoulder struck a rock, but the blow was of small moment. He came up, spluttering and still holding the paddle.

"Whe—where are you, Dave?" was his first question, as he dashed the water from his eyes.

There was no answer, and in the mist and darkness he could see nothing. He struck out, and soon reached a spot where he could stand on the rocky bottom of the watercourse. He was under some tree-limbs, and knew that the shore must be close at hand.

"I say, Dave!" he called again. "Dave!"

"Henry!" was the feeble reply.

The voice was sufficient for Henry to locate the canoe, and he hastened toward it. Feeling around in the utter darkness he caught hold of his cousin's knee and then his arm.

"What's the matter? Are you hurt?"

"I—I don't know," faltered Dave. "A tree-limb struck me on the head." He put up his hand. "Phew! I've got a lump on my forehead like a walnut!"

Henry could feel that the canoe was filling with water, and so lifted up the guns and the powder and bullet horns. Dave was slowly recovering from the shock received. Both stood up and leaned against a thick limb above the canoe.

"Let us follow the limb to shore," said Henry, and this was done, they taking everything that had been in the canoe with them.

Among the jagged rocks the water swirled swiftly, and they had to pick their way with care. Close to the tree-trunk was a deep hole, and they had to circle this. At last they stood on the shore, where the rocks were backed up by brushwood and tall timber.

"I fancy the canoe is done for," announced Dave. "It went up on those rocks good and hard."

"Well, let us be thankful that it carried us as far as it did," answered Henry, trying to be cheerful. "We must be four or five miles from that Indian camp."

"You are wet to the skin, Henry. You'll have to dry your clothes or you'll take cold."

"I'll wring them out and make that do, Dave. We won't dare to light a campfire."

"Not if we can find a hollow? The mist will hide a good deal, remember."

"Well, we'll see about it."

Henry did not relish remaining in the wet and darkness any more than did his cousin, and both searched around until they found a spot with high rocks on two sides and a thick group of trees opposite. To get some dry wood was the next task, and then came the problem of starting the blaze. But this was solved by Henry, who poured some loose powder on a dry rock, mixed it with some tinder, and then hammered the rock with the ramrod of his gun. Soon came a flash and a hiss, and the tinder glowed, and presently the fire flared up pleasantly enough. Around it they piled some flat stones, shutting in the light as much as possible.

"Do you think we ought to pull in the canoe?" asked Dave. "The Indians may come along and see it."

"It wouldn't be a bad plan," answered Henry.

They soon had the battered craft out of the river. They turned it upside down, resting each end on a rock, and thus it formed for them something of a shelter in front of the fire.

With the brightness of the blaze, matters appeared to take on a more cheerful turn. Henry took off the most of his garments and dried them, and Dave did likewise, and the former also cared for his hurt ankle. The youths calculated that it was about midnight. They did not know where they were, nor what new dangers might confront them. Each looked to his firearm, to see that it could be used if necessary, and one kept the hunting knife and the other the tomahawk in readiness.

"I think we had better take turns watching," said Henry. "There is no use in both keeping awake."

He took the first vigil, allowing Dave to sleep until about three o'clock. Then he turned in for a solid sleep lasting several hours.

In the morning the mist and the rain cleared away. The day, however, was still gloomy, and although Dave climbed one of the tall trees at hand, he could see little or nothing by which to locate himself.

"I think the fort is in that direction," he said, pointing with his hand. "But I am by no means sure."

"Well, we may as well journey in that direction as any other," was Henry's reply. "I think you are right. The canoe is not fit for use, so we cannot go down the river, and may as well throw the paddles away or burn them up."

At early dawn Dave had discovered a squirrel on a branch near by, and laid the game low with an arrow. This had made him do a little hunting with the bow, and he had ended by obtaining four squirrels. These, broiled over the fire, gave them a good breakfast, washed down as it was by a drink from the river. They looked up the watercourse as far as they could, but saw no signs of the Indians.

They were soon on the tramp. Knowing that Henry's ankle must still pain him, Dave let his cousin set the pace. This was somewhat slow for the frontier youths, but would have proved stiff walking for anybody not used to it. The route was comparatively easy to travel, and by high noon, when they sat down to rest, they calculated that they had covered at least eight miles.

"The sun is breaking through the clouds, and I am going to take another look around," said Dave, and this time Henry climbed a tree with him. A grand panorama of woods, hills, and waters was spread around them, and at a distance they saw where Fort Pitt was located, at the junction of the Allegheny and Monongahela rivers.

"There is the fort!" cried Dave, light-heartedly. "Henry we are almost on the direct road!"

"And not an Indian in sight, so far as I can see," was the answer, as Henry's trained eye moved slowly from one direction to another.

"Let us go on again. I want to get back before night—if it can be done. But, of course, you'll have to set the pace," added Dave, considerately.

As they journeyed along they talked over the situation, and wondered if the Indians had taken possession of the dead bear and her cubs.

"I don't think they took the whole bear," said Henry. "Maybe they took the hide and the choicest of the meat."

"I didn't dare to watch them too closely, for fear of being caught," said Dave.

They took an almost direct course for the fort, and by the middle of the afternoon calculated that they were but two or three miles away. Nothing had come to alarm them outside of the appearance of a rattlesnake that glided from under a rock over which they were stepping. They lost no time in giving the reptile a wide berth, and on his part the rattlesnake did not attempt to molest them.

"I think we'll reach Fort Pitt by sundown," said Henry. "We might do it in less time, but there is no use in hurrying."

"Does the ankle still hurt?"

"It doesn't hurt very much, but it feels weak. I think I'll rest all day to-morrow."

"We'll have earned a rest, I'm thinking," returned Dave, with a grim smile. "Won't they open their eyes at the fort when they hear the story we have to tell!"

Another mile was covered, and they had to pass around a hollow filled with thick brushwood. Henry was in advance, when he came to a sudden halt.

"Here is our chance, Dave!" he whispered. "We won't have to go back empty-handed."

Dave pressed to the front and took a look ahead. There, among the bushes, was a beautiful doe with a fair-sized fawn beside her.

"Good!" whispered Dave, raising his rifle. "The best kind of deer meat. Which will you take, Henry?"

"I'll take the doe."

"All right, I'll take the fawn. It's a pity to kill such a beautiful creature, but it can't be helped. We need the meat."

Both moved a little closer, to a spot where they could get a better chance at the doe and her fawn. Just as they raised their rifles the mother deer looked up and gave a sniff. The fawn followed, and both started to bound away.

Bang! bang! Both guns rang out in quick succession. The fawn fell in a heap in the bushes and lay still. The doe struggled on, mortally wounded in the breast. But hardly had she gone ten feet, with Henry and Dave after her, than an old frontiersman stepped from behind a tree, ran up, and plunged a hunting knife into her throat, bringing her career to an end.

"Sam Barringford!" cried Dave and Henry in a breath.

"Right ye air, boys," answered the old frontiersman. "I wasn't quite quick enough fer ye, was I? Thought as how thet meat war mine fer sartin."

"Were you after the doe and her fawn?" asked Henry.

"Yes—been a-followin' 'em fer the last hour. They war in sight o' the fort, an' I thought I'd add to the provender by bringin' 'em low."

"Well, you've had your hand in the killing," said Dave. He examined the fawn. "There's meat fit for the table of a king."

"Yes, and I wish mother had it," added Henry.

Sam Barringford was alone and carried only his long rifle, his horn of powder and ball, and his hunting knife. As of old he was attired in a hunting shirt, with leggings, and wore his coonskin cap, with the tail trailing behind. He was surprised to learn that they had no game with them, but still more surprised when he heard the tale they had to tell.

"We'll want to git back to the fort without delay," he said. "The commandant there must know about this."

The doe was hung on a long pole, and Dave and Henry carried the game between them. The fawn Sam Barringford slung across the back of his neck, with the front hoofs in one hand and the rear hoofs in the other. Thus they walked as swiftly as possible to the fort, where their coming was noted from a distance.

"Not so bad," said James Morris, as he eyed the game. "But you have made a long stay of it."

"Yes, and we might have had a bear, two cubs, and a buffalo had it not been for the Indians," replied Dave.

"The Indians!" burst out his parent. "Do you mean to say you ran into the Indians again?"

"We certainly did,—and I have been a prisoner, too," said Henry. "I might be a prisoner yet if it hadn't been for Dave."

"Well, this is certainly news," said Rodney. "I thought all the Indians had cleared out."

"I said all along they'd be skulkin' around," said Sam Barringford. "Don't ye remember as how I warned ye to keep your eyes peeled? Some o' them redskins ain't a goin' to git out until they actually have to, mark me!"

The news that Dave and Henry had encountered the Indians quickly spread, and Captain Ecuyer, who was in charge of the stronghold, sent for them, that he might learn the details. They knew the captain well, and readily told him all.

"I shall have to look into this," said the commandant of Fort Pitt. "The Indians must be cleared out of this district entirely."

CHAPTER VII
THE START FOR THE EAST

The news that the Indians were still in that vicinity alarmed James Morris exceedingly, and he shook his head sadly when he remembered that it had been arranged for Rodney to start for the east with little Nell and the twins on the following Monday.

"I hardly think it will be safe," said he, to Rodney. "I should not wish anything to happen to you and the others."

"There are six men to go along, besides Sam Barringford," answered the young soldier who had fought so bravely at the battle of Bushy Run. "There can be only small bodies of Indians around, and they will not dare to attack us if we keep a good watch."

"The Indians may unite for an attack," said Mr. Morris. "Better wait until we are certain the way is clear." And so the start for the Morris homestead was delayed.

Dave and Henry had returned to Fort Pitt on Friday night, and Saturday morning Captain Ecuyer sent out a body of fifty regulars and six frontiersmen, to scour the vicinity for Indians. With the number went Sam Barringford and another old hunter, Tony Jadwin, both of whom knew that territory well. Jadwin had been Mr. Morris's right-hand man at the trading post, and was counted an Indian trailer of extraordinary ability.

"I'd like to go with them myself," said Dave, but his father demurred. Henry was glad enough to give his ankle a rest, and Rodney thought he had better reserve his strength for the trip eastward.

"Oh, Henry, please don't go out among the Indians again!" cried little Nell, to her brother. "And don't you go either, Cousin Dave," she added.

"We are not going just yet," said Henry, giving his sister a kiss.

"Oh, I hate the Indians so!" went on the miss, with a stamp of her foot.

"Not all Indians," replied Dave, with a smile. "Don't forget White Buffalo."

"Oh, he is only an Indian in looks," answered Nell. "He has a white man's heart—Uncle Sam told me so."

"By the way, where is White Buffalo?" asked Henry.

"He has gone to visit his tribe," answered Rodney. "He thinks the different factions will unite now and sue for peace. Sir William Johnson is going to give them all a chance to bury the hatchet, and White Buffalo thinks it is a grand chance for his tribe to unite once more and live in peace."

What Rodney said about Sir William Johnson was true. The Indian Superintendent had sent agents to all of the chiefs of the Six Nations, and also to the chiefs of the tribes along the St. Lawrence and in Canada. The Indians were to meet the Superintendent at Johnson Hall in central New York State. Many came to the conference, which began early in September and was productive of some good, although not a great deal. The Iroquois were induced to send messages to other tribes in the west, urging them to bury the hatchet, and they also sent word to the Delawares telling them not to listen to the western tribes that desired to plunge them into further bloodshed. The Senecas would not come to the conference, and they continued to kill and plunder whenever the opportunity presented itself, and the tribes from along the Mississippi did likewise. White Buffalo's tribe of Delawares continued to remain split, much to the old chief's sorrow, one part aiding the English, and another part aiding the Indians, and the French who still held certain trading posts and refused to give them up.

The regulars and frontiersmen to sally forth from Fort Pitt after the enemy, were gone four days. When they returned they announced that practically all the red men had departed either for the north or the west. They had encountered one band of fleeing men under Moon Eye and had slain two of the Indians. One regular had been shot in the arm, a wound that was painful but not serious. They had come upon the torn carcass of the bear, which the wolves had used for a feast after the Indians had cut away the hide and some choice steaks, and had found the torn body of one cub. Sam Barringford had also gotten a long-distance shot at a buffalo, probably the one followed by Dave, but the animal had gotten away from him.

"I think we can make the trip eastward in safety now," said Rodney, to his uncle. "Evidently the redskins are pretty badly scared. It may be safer to make it now than later on. Besides, we don't want to wait till winter is on us."

The matter was talked over at great length, and finally it was decided that the start for the east should be made at the end of a week. Rodney and Barringford were to go, taking with them Nell and the twins. A settler named Dobson was also going, along with his wife, who promised to keep an eye on Nell, Tom, and Artie. The escort was to be composed of five frontiersmen, and ten regular soldiers who had received their discharge from the service, and who were anxious to get back to Annapolis, where they belonged. The party were to take with them six pack-horses, all belonging to Mr. Morris.

This plan of departing for the east put Rodney in better spirits, for he wanted to see home again, not being used to being away, as were Dave and Henry. Everything was gotten in readiness and long letters were written by those left at the fort. In his letter to his brother, James Morris stated that he intended to go back to his trading post on the Ohio as soon as it seemed fairly safe to do so, and that, as agreed upon before, he would take Dave and Henry with him.

"Good-bye, Rodney," said Dave, when it came time to part. "Take good care of yourself, and good care of Nell and the twins."

"And you take care of yourself," answered the former cripple. "Don't start for the trading post until it is perfectly safe."

When the actual parting came Nell's eyes were full of tears and she kissed her brother Henry, Uncle James, and Cousin Dave over and over again. Even the twins hated to leave the fort, where they had been general favorites since their arrival.

"Tom wants to stay by the soldiers," said one.

"Artie wants to stay by the soldiers, too, and by Dave!" cried the other.

They were sturdy little chaps, the picture of health, and Dave and Henry could not resist giving each a toss and a hug.

When the little expedition started Dave, Henry, and Mr. Morris accompanied them for several miles of the journey. Then all reached the top of a hill, and here those to remain at the fort halted. The others went on and presently a bend in the road hid them from view.

"I pray to heaven that they have a safe journey home," said James Morris, with much feeling.

As my old readers know, there were two roads running between Fort Pitt and the east—one the old trail used by General Braddock on his disastrous campaign and the other used by General Forbes on his march to victory. The Braddock road was now but little used, and Rodney and his friends took to the other, as being perhaps safer and easier.

The advance was in regular order, half of the frontiersmen and regulars going ahead and the others keeping to the rear. In the center came the pack-horses, with Rodney and Dobson in charge. With Mrs. Dobson were Nell and the twins, who walked or rode, as suited them.

In these days of fast trains, trolley cars, and automobiles it is difficult to imagine what such a journey as this before the colonists meant. Instead of covering thirty to sixty miles an hour they were content to cover ten to twenty miles between sunrise and sunset. The road lay over the hills and through the mountains, with mighty forests on all sides, where the ring of the woodsman's axe had scarcely been heard. Great rivers were to be crossed, and if the bridge was down or out of repair they had to find another place to cross or else stop to mend the structure. Where the road lay along a mountain side the rain would sometimes cover it with mud and stones to a depth of a foot or more, making the advance extra laborious. Here and there the wind had blown a tree down over their path, and then they would have to either work their way around it, or else cut through or over it. In some spots the tree-branches were so low the horses could scarcely get under them, and here all the travelers would have to advance on foot, and see to it that none of the packs were lost. Once a pack caught on a sharp bough and tore open, scattering the contents in all directions.

"Won't catch me coming out here again," grumbled Asa Dobson. "Folks out Baltimore way said I could make my fortune in them western countries, but I don't see it. Them Injuns nearly killed me and my wife twict, and they stole my hoss, and I'm going to stay in the east after this, and work for my old master, the Earl of Chester. The Injuns can have them western countries for all o' me!"

"Don't you want to be your own master and own your own plantation?" asked Rodney.

"No, not if I've got to fight Injuns to keep it," answered Dobson. He was used to life around the larger towns, and the loneliness of the wilderness struck him with a peculiar terror.

However the journey had its bright spots. The men in advance always secured plenty of game—deer, rabbits, squirrels, wild turkeys, and partridges—and the children often stopped to pick the wild flowers which still bloomed along the roadside. At nightfall they would go into camp beside some brook or spring of pure mountain water, and there would gather around a generous campfire, to eat the main meal of the day and make themselves at home. During the evening hours Sam Barringford would tell the children wonderful stories of hunting, or of his army adventures while out with Dave and Henry,—tales which they listened to with much interest.

"Tom is going to be a soldier when he grows up," said one of the little boys.

"Artie is going to be a soldier too, and have a beautiful uniform," put in the other promptly. They spoke thus in childish fashion, little dreaming of the days to come when they would both shoulder their muskets in the War for Independence.

So far they had met nobody on the road. When Sunday came they spent the day in a much-needed rest. Nell repeated to Rodney some Bible verses and tried to teach them to the twins.

On Monday afternoon those in advance saw a pack-train approaching, composed of eight horses and one cart, and in charge of six frontiersmen and a trader named Packerson.

"Where bound, Packerson?" asked Sam Barringford.

"Fort Pitt," was the short reply. Packerson was a rather silent man, of few words.

"Come straight through from Cumberland?"

"Yes."

"See any Injuns?"

"Seven. Had a fight with 'em too," answered the trader. Then his train came to a halt, and the others at once surrounded him for particulars of the encounter.

CHAPTER VIII
THE MASSACRE OF A PACK-TRAIN

Jed Packerson's story was soon told. His party had first seen the Indians while crossing a high hill where a landslide had carried down many trees of the forest to the valley below. As soon as discovered the red men had run for shelter. Half an hour later one of the frontiersmen had given the alarm, and the next moment a shower of arrows had fallen around them, hitting one man in the shoulder. Then two guns had been discharged and a horse had been hit in the thigh and had stampeded. The whites had returned the fire of the Indians, who, however, had kept under cover. At least one red warrior had been wounded, and then the whole party had taken themselves to parts unknown. The horse to run away was still missing and Packerson had decided to let him go rather than lose time on a trail that appeared so dangerous.

The fight had occurred two days before, and the spot where the Indians had opened fire was less than sixteen miles away. This was disturbing news to Rodney and his friends, and after Packerson had continued on his way a council of war was held.

"We'll have to be on our guard night an' day," said Sam Barringford. "The advance guard will have to spread out purty well an' beat the brush thoroughly. At the first sign o' danger, whistle or fire a gun and then come to the center."

The old frontiersman had been selected as a leader, and the others agreed to follow his advice. The bordermen and the regulars spread out into a regular circle around the pack-horses and those with the steeds, and Mrs. Dobson and the children were cautioned not to wander off by the roadside under any circumstances.

That evening the party encamped by the side of a stream at a point where there was a good-sized opening in the forest. Guards were stationed on both sides of the watercourse, every man being on duty four hours during the darkness. The horses were tethered in a circle and in the center a small tent was pitched, in which Mrs. Dobson, Nell, and the twins might rest.

Sam Barringford remained on guard duty from eight o'clock to midnight, his post being to the north of the camp proper, where the stream made a turn between some rocks and tall trees. The old frontiersman was tired out by his day's tramp, but did not grumble over being compelled to keep awake.

"It's got to be done, an' thet's all there are to it," he said to Rodney, "Reckon we kin sleep a week when we git to hum."

"I shan't mind staying awake, when my turn comes," answered Rodney. "But I do hope the Indians won't appear. I shouldn't care so much if we were alone, but with Mrs. Dobson, Nell, and the twins it is different."

The night was a fairly clear one, with countless stars showing between the drifting clouds. There was no breeze worth mentioning and the stillness, away from the somewhat restless horses, was intense.

Barringford walked slowly up and down the watercourse, occasionally mounting one of the rocks to get a better look at the surroundings. His trained eyes took in a good portion of territory, and the least movement among the trees would have attracted his attention. He was sleepy, but he did not allow his eyes to close for an instant.

He had just climbed down from the rocks for at least the tenth time, when he heard a rustle in some bushes at a distance. He listened with strained ears, at the same time dropping flat upon the ground, so that a possible enemy might not see him too readily.

All became silent, and he waited patiently for several minutes. Then came the crack of a twig, as some weight pressed upon it. A moment more and a figure ran through the bushes, not towards the camp but from it.

"Help!" came in a woman's voice. "Help!"

"Mrs. Dobson, by ginger!" ejaculated the old frontiersman. "What's the matter with her?"

The fleeing woman was some distance away, and he made after her with all possible speed. She crashed through the bushes and he came after her.

"Mrs. Dobson!" he called. "What is the matter? Stop!"

His cries, and those of the frantic woman, aroused the entire camp, and Dobson himself came rushing toward Barringford, followed by Rodney.

The old frontiersman soon gained the immediate rear of the woman. As he did so, he heard a rush through the thickets ahead and caught a glimpse of an Indian. Then he saw another red warrior rise up from behind a rock, tomahawk in hand. This fellow made a leap for Mrs. Dobson, but before he could use his weapon, Barringford brought his long rifle into play and the Indian pitched forward, fatally wounded in the breast. The other Indian continued to run, and so did several others who could be heard but not seen, and soon their footsteps died away in the distance.

"Maria, what is it?" cried Asa Dobson, catching his wife by the arm. "What is it?" And he gave her a shake. Then he saw her open her eyes and stare at him. "Creation! Be you asleep?" he gasped.

"Asa! Oh, save me!" she screamed. "Save me from the Indians! Don't let them scalp me!" Then she gazed around in bewilderment. "I—I thought we were at the fort and the Indians had come in after us," she faltered.

"You were dreaming," said her husband. "We are on the journey to Cumberland and Baltimore."

"Yes, yes, I know; but—but———" She stared around her. "I—I—where is the tent, and the horses?"

"You've had a nightmare, and it did us a heap o' good," broke in Sam Barringford. "Your runnin' around has scared off some redskins, I reckon."

By this time half a dozen were near. They gazed at the red warrior whom Barringford had laid low.

"He is done for," said Rodney. "He is too far gone even to question him." But even as the young soldier spoke the red man raised up suddenly and flung his tomahawk squarely at Barringford. The fling was a weak one and the weapon fell short of its mark. Then the warrior sank back, gave a gasp, and was dead.

"Game to the last," muttered Barringford. "Don't know as I blame him. Might be I'd do likewise, ef one o' the varmin plugged me," he added philosophically.

It took several minutes for Mrs. Dobson to settle herself. Her husband stated that she often arose in her sleep. She had been terribly worked up over the red men ever since leaving Fort Pitt, and this had gotten on her nerves.

The alarm kept the entire camp "on edge" until daybreak. Barringford and two others made several tours in the immediate vicinity, but could see or hear nothing more of the enemy.

"They have either cleared out entirely, or else they know how to hide," said the old frontiersman.

"Do you think it is the same party that Packerson met?" questioned Rodney.

"Like as not, Rodney. We ain't seen or heard o' anybody else on this trail."

They went on as before, and the following forenoon made a discovery that filled even the stoutest of them with horror. Coming to a spot where the road led down to a ford over a good-sized brook they beheld a man lying beside a rock, with one ear gone and part of his scalp cut away. The man was shot through the body and was all but dead.

"Who shot you?" asked one of the frontiersman, running up.

"Th—the Indians," was the low and hoarse answer. "Water!"

Water was brought, but the man was almost too weak to drink. One of the party recognized him as Stephen Banoggin, a trader well known in those days around Carlisle and Bedford. Banoggin had left Bedford ten days before, with a view of establishing a new trading post in the vicinity of Venango as soon as it seemed safe to do so.

"All dead—all killed by the Indians!" was about all he could say. "Fool, fool that I was to attempt it! All dead!" And that night he expired.

His tale was almost true, although not quite so. His pack-train had consisted of ten horses and nine men, including three negroes who were his slaves. The Indians—a mixed band under a chief called Crow Feather—had ambushed the train at the ford and slained or mortally wounded all but one negro and a white hunter named Sturm, a German from upper Pennsylvania. Sturm and the negro got away together, each however wounded. They traveled for four weeks in the forest, when Sturm went crazy. At last they reached a settlement, where the negro told his story. Sturm was placed under medical care and regained his reason some time later.

The sights presented to Rodney and the others at the ford were so revolting that Mrs. Dobson, Nell, and the twins were held back, that they might not see what had occurred. The slain were all scalped and an effort had been made to burn one at the stake. The bodies of the men and the dead horses lay together. Four horses were missing, and on these the Indians had packed such stores as they wanted, scattering the other goods or burning them.

"This is enough to make one sick!" said Rodney, as he turned away with a shudder. "These redskins must have been fiends!"

"They were certainly cold-blooded," answered Barringford. "Poor Banoggin! He had better have stayed in the east."

"Sam, this doesn't look as if it would be safe for us to go any further."

"Easily said, lad; but what are ye goin' to do?"

"You mean it is as safe to go forward as to turn back?"

"Don't it look thet way?"

"Maybe. But we are a little closer to Fort Pitt than we are to Fort Cumberland."

"Thet's true too. But I don't reckon the Injuns will dare to go as far east as Cumberland—not after the lickin' they got at Bushy Run."

"The band that did this can't be the band that tried to surround us."

"No, they are another tribe, I think."

"Then the forest must still be full of wandering bands, and we are not near as safe as we thought we were."

"We've got to make the best on't, Rodney. We must travel as fast as we can and keep our eyes peeled more'n ever before. It's the only way out, so far as I kin see."

The bodies of the slain were placed in a hollow, with some flat stones on top, to keep off the wolves and other wild beasts. The place was marked on the trees. A few of Banoggin's possessions were taken along and the others left where they had fallen.

"Poor fellow, he will never want anything in this life again," murmured Rodney, brokenly. And when the trader died they placed his body away with those of his followers. Fortunately he had been a bachelor, so there would be no widow or child to mourn his loss.

Early in the morning Rodney and those with him moved on again. Everybody in the party was exceedingly sober. All realized their great danger. The fate of Stephen Banoggin and his party was ever before their eyes and in their thoughts.

CHAPTER IX
UNDER THE CLIFF

"Thank fortune we have come so far without injury!"

It was Rodney who uttered the words. He and Sam Barringford were standing on a little rise of ground, the trail in front and behind them. The warm noonday sun shone down upon them, and all was calm and peaceful with not an enemy of any kind in sight. Close at hand Dobson and his wife were preparing a meal for all hands and little Nell was playing with the twins.

Two days had passed since they had left the fateful ford, and they had covered thirty-two miles, over a trail which the past rains had left in anything but a good condition. They had been on guard every minute, day and night, their nerves strung to top tension. The early morning had taken them through a spot lined upon either side with tall rocks, and they had expected a shot at almost every turn—but nothing had come to disturb them.

Considering the condition of the road, the horses had done well. Only one was injured,—from slipping over some rocks,—but he could still carry his load. Nobody was sick, although the constant worry had given Mrs. Dobson a headache.

"While we are waiting for dinner, let us go ahead and look at the trail," suggested Rodney; and Barringford agreed. Not far off was another hollow, backed by a cliff of rocks, overgrown with heavy vines, and they were both anxious to know what was beyond.

They gained the region of the cliff without difficulty. To save himself the trouble of climbing the rough rocks, Rodney tested the vines and then commenced to pull himself up, hand over hand.

"Be careful that you don't fall!" cried the old frontiersman. "These rocks at the bottom ain't no easy bed to drop on, I kin tell ye thet!"

"The vines are strong enough to hold a horse," answered the young soldier.

He continued to go up, until he was a good fifteen feet over Barringford's head. He had still six feet to go, when he heard a slight sound from above.

"Must be the vines tearing away," he told himself, after a pause. "Maybe they are not as strong as I thought they were."

He glanced up, saw his dire peril, and let himself drop.

He waited and then went up an additional foot or two. The vines held, and he took another grip of them a little higher up. His head was now within a yard of the top of the cliff, which was covered with the vines and a stunted growth of bushes.

Suddenly, from out of the bushes, there appeared the head of an Indian, bedecked in war-paint and feathers. Then a long, bronzed arm stole forward, holding a tomahawk. The tomahawk was raised and a blow was aimed at Rodney's head.

Had the blow fallen as intended, the young soldier's skull must have been cleft in twain. He glanced up, saw his dire peril, and let himself drop. An instant later a shot rang out from below, and the Indian's hand quivered and the hatchet slipped down among the vines and out of sight.

Rodney struck the rocks below heavily and rolled over. When he sat up he found Sam Barringford beside him, the smoke still rolling out of the frontiersman's gun.

"Oh, Sam——" he began, and knew not what further to say.

"Press in clost to the wall," answered the frontiersman, hastily, and began to reload his rifle with all speed. Rodney's gun stood against the rocks, where he had left it on starting to mount the cliff.

"Did you hit him, Sam?"

"Yes, an' I reckon I broke his wrist—leas'wise, he drapped the tomahawk. It was a narrer shave fer you, lad."

"Indeed it was." Rodney tried to catch his breath, which the sudden drop had knocked out of him. "Do you suppose he is alone?"

"Ain't supposin' nuthin jest yit. Are you all right?"

"I—think so."

Both pressed in close to the rocky wall, so that no one standing above could see them. They listened, but no sound from above reached them.

"Perhaps the Indian ran away," said Rodney, wiping the blood from where his left hand had been scratched.

"Don't be too sure, Rodney."

"If the enemy are so close we ought to warn the others."

"The rifle shot will do that. Maybe somebuddy will be comin' this way soon."

They waited another five minutes, even the old frontiersman not knowing exactly what to do. Then they saw a frontiersman named Casbury coming forward, slowly and cautiously.

"Look out!" shouted Barringford. "Injun on the rocks!" And he pointed upward.

Casbury understood, and promptly dove out of sight behind some bushes. As he did this there was a crashing through the vines, and a mass of rocks and dirt came down directly in front of where Rodney and Barringford were standing.

"Goin' to bombard us with rocks, hey?" snorted the old frontiersman. "Maybe I kin play ye a trick fer that. Groan, Rodney, groan," and he began to groan and moan, as if in the greatest of pain. Rodney did the same, keeping it up several minutes. Then both began to breathe heavily, as though totally exhausted.

Several minutes more passed and Rodney and Barringford breathed softer and softer. Thrown off their guard, and thinking the whites dead or mortally hurt, three Indians leaned over the edge of the cliff to get a view of the situation.

The young soldier and the old frontiersman were on the alert, and as soon as the warriors appeared they blazed away. Two drew back, one with a shot through the side of the neck. The third pitched forward with a yell, struck the rocks head first, and lay dead where he had landed.

"There, I reckon thet will teach 'em a lesson," cried Sam Barringford, as he and Rodney again loaded up.

A shot was now fired by Casbury, and another Indian was hit in the shoulder. Then Casbury saw four Indians run from the front of the cliff and disappear in the bushes far back.

"Come on, if you want to!" cried Casbury, and leaving the shelter of the cliff Rodney and Barringford made for the camp with all haste. Here they found all the others on guard. The midday meal was forgotten, and the men stood ready to shoot the moment a red warrior showed himself.

"This is the worst possible place to be caught in," said Rodney. "The Indians can get behind yonder trees and pick us off at will—if they have any firearms."

"I saw nothing but bows and arrows," said Casbury. "Still, they may have guns."

The situation was talked over while they waited for the Indians to reappear. Some brushwood had been gathered for the fire, and Mrs. Dobson and the children were placed behind this and behind some of the horses.

"I'm going over into the woods," said Barringford, to the others. "If I see anything wrong, I'll screech like an owl."

"Do you want me to go along?" asked Rodney.

"No, lad, I want you to stay here, by Nell an' the twins."

Barringford slipped to the rear, crawled through the grass, and thus reached a few low bushes, from which he made his way into the forest.

Two hours went by slowly. Not an Indian showed himself, nor did any signal come from Barringford. The men remained on the alert, and when a rabbit crossed the trail two drew a bead on the animal like a flash.

"I trust Sam hasn't gotten into trouble," said Rodney, at last.

"If he has, he'll have to git out o' it," answered one of the others, with a shrug of his shoulders.

Presently one of the regulars saw a form wriggling through the grass. He was on the point of firing when he recognized the old frontiersman. Barringford came in a good deal out of breath.

"We've got to move, an' move quick, too!" he announced. "There's a crowd o' thirty Injuns over thar,"—he pointed with his hand. "They are goin' to attack us as soon as the sun goes down."

"But where shall we move to?" questioned Rodney.

"I war thinkin' o' thet cave ye spoke about, Hempser," went on Barringford, turning to one of the other old hunters. "You said it war nigh here."

"It's half a mile beyond the cliff," was Hempser's answer. "I don't know the way very good, but I think I can find it."

"Then thet is where we'll go, an' to onct," decided Sam Barringford.

Not a minute was lost in breaking camp, and in a close body the pack-train set out, past the cliff and then through a valley of heavy grass and bushes. The men carried their guns ready for use, and screened Mrs. Dobson and the children as much as possible.

"Oh dear! I'd rather be dead than be so worried," sighed the woman. "I am that nervous I am ready to drop!"

At the end of the short valley was another rise of rocks, among which was located the cave. They had just gained the first of the rocks when a hideous war-whoop sounded out on the afternoon air.

"They have discovered us!" cried Rodney, and he was right. At the far end of the valley appeared fully a score of Indians, a few on horseback and the others on foot.

The Indians had been surprised, thinking the whites were still on the trail. But they soon recovered, and came riding and running towards our friends, yelling at the top of their lungs and flourishing their tomahawks. A moment later they sent a volley of arrows and several rifle shots, for some carried one kind of weapon and some the other.

"Are you hurt?" asked Barringford of Rodney, as he saw the young soldier stagger.

"No, an arrow hit me in the coat-sleeve, that's all—it didn't get through my shirt though."

One of the regulars had been struck by a bullet in the shoulder, and his friends had to help him along. Then the Indians sent forth more arrows, one of which tore through little Nell's dress.

"Oh!" cried the little miss, in great terror.

"Give 'em a dose o' their own medicine!" ordered Barringford. "Make the shots tell!" And then everybody fired at the advancing foe, and three of the red warriors pitched into the grass, while two others stopped running and then limped to the rear, badly wounded.

Hempser was looking around anxiously for the cave. At first he could not locate it, but, just as the Indians advanced again, he discovered a hole and rushed towards it.

"Here you are!" he shouted. "This way! Once in the cave, I think we can hold 'em at bay!"

"Into the cave!" cried Barringford. "Mrs. Dobson and the children first. Hempser, is there a back opening?"

"Yes, but not a very big one. We can close it up with loose rocks."

"Then you run back and pile up the rocks. The others remain at this opening, to keep the Indians at a distance."

CHAPTER X
BARRINGFORD AS A SCOUT

The volley poured into the Indians by the whites made the red warriors pause for the time being. They were close to a clump of bushes and trees growing near the center of the glade, and they got behind this shelter with alacrity.

In the cave all was confusion. It was an opening ten to fifteen feet in height and equally broad at the mouth. It ran back a distance of over two hundred feet, where it ended in a split among the rocks, coming out at a point where there was a thick patch of nettle bushes.

The horses had been brought into the cave and were led to the rear. Here Hempser worked like a Trojan, with one of the regulars helping him. Loose stones were to be had in plenty, and they blocked up the rear opening completely.

"They'll have their hands full, getting in this way," said the regular. "The nettles will keep them back if nothing else will."

"Right you are," answered Hempser. "Injuns don't like to git scratched any more than anybody else."

At the front of the cavern Sam Barringford took command. A glance showed him how the land lay, and he at once ordered some of the men to pile up the loose stones to a height of several feet. This formed a barricade, behind which the frontiersmen and regulars could lie with but little danger of the enemy picking them off.

"This is a situation we didn't bargain for," said Rodney, after the construction of the barricade had come to an end. "I must say I don't like it."

"Well, lad, it's better than being surrounded in the open," answered Barringford, with an effort to look on the bright side of the affair.

"I don't think they'll attack us now," went on the young soldier. "But they may do it to-night."

"We'll have to keep on guard, and shoot the first man who shows himself," put in Casbury.

"Maybe they'll try to starve us out," came from another of the frontiersman.

"We've got rations enough for a week or more, on a pinch," said Rodney. "We've got our regular things and also that deer Barton shot early this morning, and some rabbits."

"How about water?" asked another.

"We'll have to see about that," said Sam Barringford.

Satisfied that the Indians did not contemplate an immediate attack, the old frontiersman, accompanied by Rodney, made a tour of the cave, lighting a torch for that purpose. In one corner the rocks were found to be very damp, and when some were pulled up a little water trickled forth.

"Thar's a spring thar," said Barringford, with satisfaction. "We kin do a bit o' diggin' an' then have all the water we wish." A little later two of the regulars set to work, with pike-poles and shovels, and soon had a hollow made into which the water flowed to a depth of several inches. The water was brought up in a dipper, and proved to be both clear and wholesome.

As the time slipped by the whole party became more composed, and Nell and the twins clamored for their delayed dinner. A meal was prepared in the cave, which the men ate while on the watch.

"Oh, Rodney, will the bad Indians catch us in here?" asked Nell, as she came up to her elder brother.

"I think not, Nell," he answered, hopefully.

"I wish I was home."

"So do I, Nell—wish it more for your sake than for my own."

"Tom wants to go out and fight the bad Indians," said one of the twins. He had picked up a rifle resting against the wall and was trying to shoulder the long weapon.

"Here, you give me that gun!" cried Rodney, reaching for it. "Tom, you mustn't play with the guns. One of 'em might go off and hurt you."

"Tom ain't 'fraid of no gun," said the little boy. "Want to shoot the Indians."

"You keep quiet and stay with Mrs. Dobson or Nell."

"How long will we have to stay here, Rodney?" asked his little sister.

"I can't answer that question, Nell. It depends on the Indians. Perhaps they'll get tired of watching us and go away."

It was a hard matter to keep the twins quiet, but presently both grew tired of wandering around the cave, and went to sleep on a pair of blankets spread out for them. Mrs. Dobson sat on one of the packs with Nell beside her and her husband not far off.

"Oh, Asa, how foolish we were to come out to this western country!" sighed the woman, for at least the fiftieth time. "We should have stayed at home and been content with what we had!"

"Ain't no uset to cry over spilt milk," grumbled her husband.

"I think the Indians will come to-night and scalp all of us!"

"Oh, Mrs. Dobson, you don't mean that!" gasped little Nell.

"Don't scare the little girl, Mrs. Dobson," put in Casbury, who chanced to be near. "It won't help matters to git anybuddy worked up."

At last the sun sank in the west and it began to grow dark at the mouth of the cave. Two men were stationed at the spot where the rear opening had been, and all the others gathered at the front. Then Sam Barringford called Rodney to him.

"I'm a-goin' out on a scoutin' tour," said the old frontiersman. "I'm a-goin' to leave you an' Casbury in charge until I git back. Don't shoot me, but don't let none o' them Injuns git near, nuther."

"Don't you want me to go with you, Sam?"

"No, it will be hard enough fer one to git around, let alone two. Ef ye ain't sure it's me comin' back, hoot like an owl an' I'll answer like a catbird, understand?"

"Yes."

Barringford gave the others a few directions and then, stepping quickly over the rocks, snaked his way along through the grass to a fringe of low bushes. From the bushes he made for the rough rocks, where he paused, to consider the situation in all of its details.

The old frontiersman felt that he was surrounded by enemies fully as alert as himself and ready to shoot him down on sight.

"An' they won't ax me if I'll like it nuther," he murmured to himself. "They be jest a-hankerin' arter my sculp like all possessed."

Peering cautiously around, he saw nobody, and after a short wait took his way between the rocks towards the spot where the rear of the cave was located. Here he listened again, and this time heard the low murmur of two voices. But they were those of Dobson, the settler, and a regular, talking from inside.

"They ought to know enough to keep quiet," mused the old frontiersman, in disgust. "How can they spot the enemy if they gab like thet?"

In a few minutes the voices ceased, and thinking the coast clear the old frontiersman worked his way among the rocks and through the bushes toward a point he imagined the Indians might be holding. The darkness of night had now fallen completely over the forest and scarcely a sound broke the stillness.

Barringford was about to cross to another patch of brushwood when the distant call of a night bird arrested his attention. He was well versed in the calls of all birds and that which he heard did not sound exactly true to his ear. He smiled grimly to himself and waited.

As he had surmised, an answering call soon followed. It came from the very brushwood he had been on the point of entering, and a tall Indian stepped forth, as if to advance. Before Barringford could retreat or draw to one side the pair were face to face.

Not a word was uttered—indeed, there was no time for speech. The Indian had his tomahawk in his hand, and this he raised, aiming a blow at the old frontiersman's skull. As old as he was getting, Barringford was still nimble on his feet and dexterously dodged to one side. As the arm of the red warrior came down, he caught the red man by the shoulder, and over went the pair on the soil. Then the Indian tried to cry out, but Barringford's hand was clapped on his mouth.

It now became a desperate but silent struggle for life. From the red man's mouth, the old frontiersman's hand was shifted to his throat, which was caught with a grip of steel. The Indian struggled desperately, first kicking heavily and then drawing up a knee against Barringford's breast. Then he tried to use his tomahawk again, and hit the frontiersman a glancing blow on the shoulder. The hatchet fell, and in a twinkling the Indian had Barringford by the throat, in a clutch equally firm and relentless.

Like two bulldogs that have a death-grip and will not let go, white man and Indian rolled over and over, on the rocks and in the bushes, each doing all in his power to get the better of the other. The Indian was muscular, and his strength was equal if not superior to that of his white adversary. But Barringford had secured the first grip, and the red man's breath was fast leaving him. His tongue stuck out, his eyes bulged from their sockets, and he could not utter even so much as a faint gurgle.

It was at this moment that an interruption came. Another form glided into the midst of the bushes. It was a second Indian, and a glance showed him the condition of affairs. Without stopping to use his tomahawk or his knife he kicked Barringford heavily in the left ear. Then followed other blows, and with a groan the old frontiersman stretched out on the rocks unconscious.

As the hold on his throat relaxed the Indian who had been in the death struggle gave a gasp and stared about him. The coming of his fellow warrior had undoubtedly saved his life.

"Where did that white man come from?" asked the second Indian, as he gave Barringford a close look.

"Cushina knows not," was the faint reply. It was some time before the other could get back his breath.

"Are there others about?"

At this question Cushina shrugged his shoulders.

"Did he come from the cave, think you?"

"Perhaps—all of the whites were driven to that shelter, like so many dogs of the prairie."

"It may not be so. Others may be at hand. We must be careful. Moon Eye has news of some soldiers. They may be marching in this direction."

"Then Moon Eye himself is here?"

"Yes."

The first warrior drew a long breath and then brought from his girdle a keen hunting knife. He felt of its edge with satisfaction.

"Mist of the Lake has come to the aid of Cushina and has brought the white man to grief," said he, looking at the other closely. "Does Mist of the Lake claim the scalp?"

At this query the second Indian shrugged his shoulders.

"Does Cushina still wish to linger in the footsteps of Laughing Eyes and make her his bride?" he asked, after another pause.

Cushina winced at this question. Both he and Mist of the Lake were in love with the same Indian maiden. As Mist of the Lake had saved his life he was bound, according to the laws of his tribe, to give his rival a clear field in his wooing.

"Laughing Eyes is Mist of the Lake's—if she will have him," he said, in a low voice.

"And the scalp of the white man belongs to Cushina," was the prompt reply of the other warrior. "He can take it at his pleasure."

CHAPTER XI
IN WHICH WHITE BUFFALO APPEARS

"Something must surely have happened to Sam, or he wouldn't stay away as long as this," said Rodney to Casbury, after half the night had passed without the old frontiersman reappearing.

"I am afraid you are right, Rodney. Maybe the Injuns caught an' killed him."

"Don't you think somebody ought to go out and try to hunt him up?"

"It won't be any safer for us than it was for him," answered the borderman, with a grave shake of his head.

Had it not been for Nell and the twins Rodney might have gone on a hunt for his old friend. But he felt his responsibility, and so remained in the cavern. He felt that if an attack came his place was beside his sister and the twins. Barringford thought as much of the twins as if they were his own flesh and blood, and would not forgive him did he not do all he could to shield the youngsters from harm.

Slowly the time wore away. Nell, the twins, and Mrs. Dobson had gone to sleep, and also several of the frontiersmen and regulars, who were off duty for the time being. The cave was kept in total darkness, so that those inside could see better what was happening without.

Rodney had listened for the cry of a catbird in vain, and stood leaning against a rock, peering forth into the semi-darkness. He was tremendously sleepy, having gotten only a short nap the night before.

Presently he straightened up and listened. Was he mistaken, or had he heard the croaking of a frog? He had not noticed this earlier in the night.

He was not mistaken; the croaking was repeated, at regular intervals. He could not resist the temptation to croak also, mimicking the sound as best he could. At once the answer came back, and the heart of the young soldier gave a bound of astonishment and gratification.

The call was one often used by White Buffalo, the old chief of the Delawares who had proved such a friend to the different members of the Morris family. What he could be doing in this vicinity was a mystery, since it was supposed that he was either at the regular village of his tribe or at the conference being held by Sir William Johnson and the red men at Johnson Hall.

"Perhaps it's a ruse," thought Rodney. "I must be on my guard—it won't do to be caught in a trap."

The croaking of the frog continued, moving gradually closer to the mouth of the cave. Then Rodney saw something wave in the air, between two bushes.

The object went up and down twice, then crosswise three times and then around in a circle.

"White Buffalo true enough!" murmured the young soldier. He called some of the others to his side. "White Buffalo, a friendly Indian, is out there. He wants to talk to us."

"I'll trust none of them," said one of the regulars promptly. "They are all cutthroats!"

"White Buffalo has been a friend to our family for years," went on the young soldier. "I can vouch for him in every respect. You know him, Casbury, and so do you, Malloy."

"Yes, he is square, so far as I know," answered Casbury.

"He's a putty good Indian, so he is," said the Irish borderman mentioned. "But not wan av thim can be thrusted whin the war's goin' ag'in 'im. Betther be afther bein' careful, Rodney."

"He wants to talk to us—he has something important to say," persisted Rodney.

"How do yez know that?"

"He just signaled to me. He and my brother Henry and cousin Dave are great friends, and White Buffalo taught us some of his signals. We had better let him come in and talk to us."

Those in the cave discussed the matter and at last agreed to follow Rodney's advice. But they remained on guard, to shoot White Buffalo or any other Indian down, at the first sign of treachery.

The matter settled, Rodney signaled White Buffalo to approach. He started to go forth, to meet the friendly red man, but White Buffalo quickly warned him back. In a minute the old Delaware chief was in the cavern.

"White Buffalo, I am glad to see you," cried Rodney, shaking hands.

"How! how!" returned the aged Indian. He peered closely at Rodney in the darkness. "My friend Rodney is better? He can walk well?"

"Yes, I am much better. And how are you? Hello, there is blood on your face!"

"White Buffalo had a fight—down by the river—with some other Indians. They had almost killed his old friend Barringford."

"Sam! Is he alive?"

"Yes—White Buffalo knocked an Indian over. Then he took Sam and ran through the forest. They were about to torture Sam—to make him speak of this place and who was here. First one Indian wanted his scalp, but Moon Eye came up and stopped the bloody work."

"And you fought the Indians alone?"

"No, White Buffalo has six warriors with him—they are watching down at the river. Sam could not come—he is too sorely wounded. He sent White Buffalo. He told White Buffalo to cry as a catbird, but that is a bad signal—it would bring Moon Eye and his warriors to the spot. So White Buffalo used the old signal—the one he taught to Dave and Henry. He thought his friend Rodney would remember."

"And I did remember. But you are hurt. Let me bind up the wound."

"'Tis but a scratch," answered the aged Indian. The cut smarted greatly, but he would not show his pain.

"See here, what do you know about the other Indians around here?" asked Casbury.

"They number thirty," said White Buffalo, who had learned how to count in English style. "All strong, crafty, and full of the war spirit. White Buffalo's small band can do but little against them."

In his own fashion the Indian then told his story in detail, how he and his followers were journeying to a distant village, to try to bring their entire tribe in harmony with each other. They had seen the actions of Moon Eye and his followers while at a distance and come to the conclusion that something unusual was going on. They had come closer and heard the other Indians discuss the subject of an attack on the cave. The followers of Moon Eye intended to wait until daybreak and then try to smoke out those in the place. All the men were to be shot down and scalped, and the woman and the children were to be made captives. This much White Buffalo had learned before going to the rescue of Sam Barringford. What Moon Eye and his men were going to do now, the old chief could not tell.

"What do you think we had best do?" asked Rodney, after the recital had come to an end.

"Escape from the cavern without delay," answered the aged Indian. "'Tis the only hope. Unless that is accomplished you will surely be shot down like bears coming from a smoke-out."

"How shall we go?"

"If you will trust yourselves to White Buffalo he will do what he can," answered the old chief, simply.

Rodney was willing, and some of the others said they would follow the chief, but several of the regulars demurred and so did Malloy the frontiersman.

"I'll thrust meself to no redskin," said the Irishman, with a vigorous shake of his head. "I have no desire to wake up in the marnin' wid me throat cut!"

"I shall follow White Buffalo," said Rodney, decidedly. "And I shall take Nell and Tom and Artie with me."

"White Buffalo is a good Indian!" cried Nell, who had awakened and run forward to greet the old chief, whom she knew by the voice. "I know he will save me," and she took his hand confidently.

At last Malloy and the regulars gave in and all looked to see what White Buffalo's first move would be. His plan to rescue them was as old as it was simple.

"White Buffalo will go back to his braves," said the aged chief. "They will make a great noise to the northward, fire shots and yell. They will attack one or two of Moon Eye's men. That will cause Moon Eye to rush with more warriors to that point. Then my friends must slip away in the darkness and go down to the river—to the spot where Sam has been left. I will tell how the spot can be found." And he did so.

This matter arranged, White Buffalo added that he and his braves would join the whites in the morning—the signal to be the croaking of frogs. Then, after a few additional words to Rodney, he bowed to those around him, leaped over the barricade of stones, and vanished into the night.

No time was lost, after the departure of the aged Indian chief, in getting ready to leave the cave. Such things as could be dispensed with were left behind. Two horses were brought to the front, and Nell and Tom were placed on one and Mrs. Dobson and Artie on another. All the men looked to their firearms and their hunting knives.

"This may be our last night on earth," said one regular. "At the best, we have only a fighting chance."

Casbury had followed White Buffalo and was outside, on the watch. He fancied that he saw an Indian at a distance, but was not sure and did not fire.

A half-hour went by—an unusually long time to those in the cavern, whose nerves were strung to the topmost pitch. All was now in readiness for the flight, but so far not a sound had broken the stillness.

"Mebbe something has miscarried," observed one regular.

"White Buffalo may be dead," said another. "One of the Moon Eye crowd may have been lying in wait for him."

A few minutes more passed, and even Rodney was beginning to worry, when from a distance came a rifle shot. Then arose a mad yelling, and more shots were fired. The din increased, until the alarm appeared to spread through the whole of the forest to the north of the cave. White Buffalo and his six trusty followers were making noise enough for a band of fifty, and it must be confessed that Moon Eye and his warriors were taken completely by surprise.

"'Tis the Delawares!" was the cry. "They have come to do us battle!"

"Mist of the Lake has been killed!" called out another. "And Squat Foot is wounded!"

The din kept on, and for the time being the attention of all the Indians was taken from the cavern. This was what Rodney had hoped for, and as soon as he thought it safe, he ordered an advance. The men rushed out of the cave and, finding the coast clear, urged forward the horses, and away went the whole expedition into the woods to the south of the cavern.

"There is one Injun!" cried an old frontiersman.

"Don't shoot—unless it becomes necessary!" said Rodney, hastily, as the man raised his rifle. "If we can get away silently, so much the better."

The Indian had only his bow and arrows with him. He did not stop to attack the whites, but ran into the forest,—to join those moving to the north. He, like the others, imagined that a large band of their hated rivals, the Delawares, had appeared.

Rodney kept as close as possible to the horses on which rode Mrs. Dobson and the children. On the other side was Asa Dobson, in such a tremble that he could scarcely walk. The settler imagined that every minute might be his last.

"I'd give all my money to be back home again!" he groaned.

"Money doesn't count here," said Rodney, briefly. "We must use our wits, and if the worst comes to the worst, fight to the last,—for the sake of your wife and the children!"

CHAPTER XII
HOME ONCE MORE

The route to the river was a rough one, over jagged rocks and around stunted growths of evergreens and elderberry bushes, with here and there a bramble bush or a tangle of wild grapes. Often the men stumbled, and it was with difficulty that the horses got through without throwing their loads.

Not a word was spoken, Rodney cautioning all to silence. Every eye and ear was on the alert. Who knew but what they might be running into an ambush of the worst kind?

When the watercourse was gained,—a small stream flowing to the southeastward,—they came to a halt in a small grove of hemlocks and walnuts. Not another Indian had appeared, for which all were thankful.

The din to the northward was now growing less, and Rodney was certain that White Buffalo and his handfuls of braves were in retreat, not daring to meet the superior force under Moon Eye.

On gaining the vicinity his Indian friend had mentioned to him, Rodney lost no time in looking around for Sam Barringford.

"Sam!" he called, softly. "Sam, are you here?"

"Rodney!" came in a weak voice. "Here I be—an' glad ye have come!"

The old frontiersman was up in a short, wide-spreading tree, where White Buffalo and another friendly red man had placed him. He was weak from his encounter with the enemy and glad to have the young soldier and the others come to his aid.

"I had what ye might call a putty clost shave," said Barringford. "They got me down an' one o' the rascals war a-goin' to sculp me when Moon Eye cuts in an' says to let me alone—he would torture me into tellin' em' some o' the white folks' secrets—about the fort an' the soldiers on the march, an' sech. They war a-goin' to burn me at a stake—jest as them Injuns war goin' to burn me when I war on my way to Detroit with Dave,—when White Buffalo plays a trick on 'em."

"What did he do, Sam?"

"Got one o' his followers to wave a torch from some rocks. The feller war kivered with a white blanket an' I reckon they took him fer a ghost. When Moon Eye's crowd war lookin' at the figger in white, White Buffalo come up to me, fixed up as one o' the enemy, an' cuts me loose. I didn't know him myself till he spoke. The disguise did the trick, and we got away into the forest. Then I dropped, I war thet weak, and they brung me here. Then he said he would do what he could fer ye—an' he must have kept his word, or ye wouldn't be here," concluded the old frontiersman.

White Buffalo had mentioned another spot—down the river—where the party of whites might wait until morning for the Delawares to join them. Helping Sam Barringford upon one of the horses that had been carrying supplies, they set off for the place mentioned, reaching it without mishap just as day was breaking.

By this time the entire party was so worn out that half the number were glad to throw themselves down to rest, leaving the others on guard for two hours, when they were relieved by their companions. A light breakfast was served, no campfire being lit for fear the smoke might attract the attention of the enemy.

It was well toward noon when White Buffalo came in, he and his followers having had to make a wide detour, in order to escape another encounter with Moon Eye. White Buffalo had been struck in the left forearm by a tomahawk, an ugly but not a serious cut, and one brave had received an arrow in the fleshy part of the leg.

"Do you think they are coming this way?" was Rodney's first question.

"There is no telling what they will do next," answered the aged Indian chief. "White Buffalo and his followers drew them as far northward as possible— we could do no more. Rodney had better travel eastward as fast as he can. In that direction alone lies safety."

Without delay the march was once more begun, first to a fording spot across the stream and then directly eastward. They moved onward until long after sunset, covering at least fifteen miles, over a broken deer trail that was rough in the extreme. On the way one horse—that carrying Nell and little Tom— stepped into a hole and went down, throwing both children into the bushes.

"Are you hurt, Nell?" asked Rodney, rushing up in alarm.

"I—I think not!" she gasped. "But I don't like such tumbles at all!"

"Bad horse, to go down with Tom," said the little boy.

"He couldn't help it," answered Rodney. "I am glad you are not injured," he added, heartily, and picked the boy up in his arms while Nell arose unaided.

The horse was in a bad way, having broken his leg and dislocated his shoulder. To put him out of his misery, Rodney had one of the Indians kill him with several blows from a tomahawk. Then Nell and Tom were placed on another horse, and the party went on as before.

The next day found them once more on the regular road. Not a sign of the enemy had been seen and all began to breathe a little easier.

"I think we are out of it at last," said Rodney. "We are getting pretty well on to the east now."

"Right you are," answered Casbury.

"That White Buffalo is a pretty good Injun after all, so he is," admitted Malloy.

They had now reached what in past years had been the foremost of the homesteads along the army road. The places were burned down without exception, only the blackened ruins showing where log cabins and stables had stood. The owners had long since either fled or been killed.

"It may be a long while before this is settled again," said Rodney.

"Perhaps not, lad," answered one of the frontiersmen. "As soon as it is known the Indians are under control some folks will come out again, and others will follow," and this proved to be true. Inside of three years there were more settlements along the Forbes and the Braddock roads than ever before.

Feeling themselves fairly free from danger, they did not push along quite so rapidly. This rested the horses and was also more comfortable for Sam Barringford, who had suffered more than he cared to admit.

"Rodney will not want White Buffalo any more," said the aged chief one morning, when they were within two days' journey of Fort Cumberland. "White Buffalo must go elsewhere."

"Won't you come home with me?" asked the young soldier. "Father will be glad to see you, I know."

"White Buffalo must attend to the affairs of his tribe," was the reply, and soon the aged chief departed with his followers, stating that if it was possible he would stop at Fort Pitt and let James Morris, Dave, and Henry know how they had come through without great loss. Rodney thanked the Indian for all he had done and shook hands warmly, and Barringford did the same. It was a long while, and many startling things occurred, before they saw White Buffalo again.

The thoughts of Rodney and his sister turned homeward now, and both were anxious to see the old homestead once more. The twins did not remember much, having been away so long, but they were glad to get away from "the shooting Indians" as Artie called them.

It was a cold but clear day when the expedition reached Fort Cumberland. Here the regulars reported, as they had been told to do, and were properly discharged from further service in the army. Rodney, Barringford, and the others also told their stories and delivered a message sent by Colonel Bouquet, who was still near Fort Pitt, trying to locate Pontiac.

All was now comparatively quiet around Fort Cumberland. To the southward, a small band of Indians had appeared a few weeks before and attacked some white and colored people, carrying two colored girls, slaves of a Mr. Bowman, into captivity. To the northward, the enemy had fallen on a band of Moravians while at their devotions and slaughtered one of the leaders and two young women. The Moravians were very bitter and wanted the English army to drive the red men to the far west, beyond the Mississippi.

Leaving the others at Fort Cumberland, Rodney took the horses and set off for the Morris homestead, in company with Barringford, Nell, and the twins. The route was now familiar even to Nell, and she watched eagerly for the first sign of the cabin.

"Papa! I see papa!" she cried, as they made a turn along the brook road, and soon they saw Joseph Morris walking toward them, rifle in hand, for none of the settlers thought of going out without being armed.

"Rodney! and Nell!" burst from Joseph Morris's lips, and he came running up with a beaming face. He kissed his little daughter several times. "Glad you are back! And you too, Sam," he added to the old frontiersman. "And how are the twins?" and he chucked them under the chin.

"I am glad to be back," said Rodney. "It seems like an age since I went away and joined the soldiers."

They did not stop to tell their story, for it was only a step more to the log cabin. Mrs. Morris, the kindest of motherly women, came rushing out of the door to greet them.

"Nell, my Nell!" she burst out, and hugged her daughter over and over again, while the tears of joy streamed down her face. "Oh, how glad I am that you are back!"

"And I am glad too, mamma," said Nell. "Oh, it's been such a very, very long time since the Indians took me!"

"And Rodney!" went on Mrs. Morris, kissing his sunburnt cheek. "How did you stand it? Didn't the old lameness bother you?" And then she hugged the twins and shook hands with Sam Barringford. It was indeed a happy meeting all around.

"You must stay home, at least for the winter," said Joseph Morris to his son. "You have seen enough of peril for a time."

"I am willing to stay home," said Rodney. "But I think I ought to join Uncle Jim and Dave and Henry in the spring."

He told all the news that evening, sitting around the kitchen fire, and Barringford and little Nell also told their tales. The old frontiersman wanted to know if any letter had come from England regarding the twins.

"Nothing as yet," said Joseph Morris. "But it is something to know that their father's name is Maurice Hamilton, and that he is well-to-do. Some day we shall probably hear from him."

Much about the homestead had been destroyed by the Indians, but Joseph Morris had worked hard to get things into shape again. Family stores had been brought in, from Fort Cumberland and from Annapolis, and the settler had cut a pile of wood for winter use.

"I hope all goes well with those left at Fort Pitt," said Joseph Morris. "It is said here that the Indians are very bitter out there."

"They certainly are," answered Rodney.

"It's a pity Pontiac was not slain. He is the head and front of this constant fighting. More than likely he will try to get up another conspiracy before long."

"Your neighbor, Jack Spader, just told me some news," said Sam Barringford, who sat on the doorstep, taking his ease in the sunshine. "It is reported at Fort Cumberland that the Indians are going to make another attack on Fort Pitt. Nobody seems to know where the report started."

"I trust it is not true," replied Rodney.

"So do I," added Mrs. Morris, "for the sake of Henry, and your uncle, and Cousin Dave."

"Well, they will have to do what they can to take care of themselves," said Joseph Morris. "Perhaps we shall have our own hands full here this winter. The Indians have made no preparations for cold weather, and rather than starve they may attack us."

CHAPTER XIII
AN OLD ENEMY APPEARS

After the departure of Rodney, Nell, and the twins from Fort Pitt, matters at that stronghold went along smoothly for several weeks. Once Dave and Henry went out hunting with Mr. Morris, and managed to secure a deer and some smaller game, but that was all.

In the meantime the meeting that Sir William Johnson had arranged with the Six Nations and other tribes of Indians from upper New York and from Canada came to a conclusion. Many of the red men agreed to keep the peace and some even agreed to take up arms against the Indians of the Mississippi region, being offered good pay for this service. But others, including the Senecas, went away murmuring, saying that the English were trying to rob them of their lands and they would not submit to it. Then there were certain bands, like that under Moon Eye, that had become absolutely lawless, killing and plundering whenever the opportunity offered. Some of these bands united with some of the most lawless of the French, especially those who held isolated trading posts, and what they did to make life miserable for the frontiersmen will be told later on.

The coming of winter in the vicinity of Fort Pitt made hunting extra good, and both Dave and Henry urged Mr. Morris to go out again. As a result a party of five was organized, the two others being Tony Jadwin the frontiersman and another character well known to my old readers, Peaceful Jones, who had fought so bravely when the Morrises had defended their trading post the season previous.

The party took along something in the way of a camping outfit and expected to be gone at least three days. Although he did not tell those at the fort, James Morris decided to push westward, to note if the way was clear, so he might start for his trading post in the spring.

The first day out the party got on the trail of a whole herd of deer. But something scared the timid creatures, and they bounded away to the westward, through a thick snow that was falling at the time.

"Oh, we must get some of those deer!" cried Henry. "We can't afford to miss them!"

"Well, we'll get them if the falling snow doesn't put us off the trail," answered his uncle.

But the snow continued to come down heavily, and by nightfall the chase had to be abandoned, at least for the time being. They went into camp between the hemlocks, finding a comfortable shelter under some thick, snow-laden branches.

"I wonder if there are any Indians around?" remarked Dave, while they were eating supper. "I hope not."

"It is possible some of them may be out hunting like ourselves," answered his father. "Somebody will have to stand guard."

But the night passed without interruption. In the morning it began to snow once more, and this time so furiously that they did not know what to do.

"Hunting is all out of the question in sech a storm as this," said Tony Jadwin, with a deep sigh. "No game stirring, onless it's a rabbit, an' they ain't wuth wastin' powder an' shot on."

The snow kept up until noon and was then over a foot in depth. But after that the sun came out, making the landscape dazzling white.

The party was coming out of a heavy stretch of timber when James Morris called a sudden halt. At a distance could be seen the smoke of a campfire.

"Must be Injuns," was Peaceful Jones's comment.

A brief consultation was held, and Tony Jadwin took it on himself to go forward and investigate. He skirted the clearing and passed among the trees, and that was the last the others saw of him for a full half-hour.

"Got news fer ye," he said, to James Morris, on returning. "Powerful news, too."

"What is it?" demanded the trader, quickly.

"Who do ye reckon I see over yonder?"

"Some Indians?"

"Yes, a handful. But thet ain't all. I see thet good-fer-nuthin' Frenchman thet made so much trouble fer ye fer years."

"What, you don't mean Jean Bevoir!" broke in Dave.

"Thet's exactly the pusson I do mean."

"I shouldn't think he'd dare to show his face around here," said Henry. "He must know that if he is captured it will go hard with him."

"An' thet ain't the whole o' it," went on Tony Jadwin. "Do ye remember thet Frenchman as run away from Fort Pitt—the feller thet had somethin' to do with stealin' them twins?"

"You mean Benoit Vascal?" asked the trader.

"Yes. Wall, he's thar too, an' he an' Bevoir seem to be putty thick, ez near ez I kin figger it."

"Father, we ought to try to capture 'em both!" burst out Dave.

"That's the talk," said Henry. "Why, it will never be safe around the trading post as long as Jean Bevoir is at large. He will incite other Frenchmen and also Indians to do us harm."

"Who else is in the party?" asked James Morris of Jadwin.

"Two other Frenchmen—trappers who used to help Bevoir—and about a dozen Injuns—the crowd that used to be under Flat Nose."

"Yes, I remember that crowd," said Dave. "They were certainly a bloodthirsty set."

"Sixteen all told," mused James Morris. "I am afraid they are too many for us."

"Perhaps the Indians won't fight," suggested Henry.

"They'll fight right enough," answered Tony Jadwin. "They have just enough rum in them to make 'em ugly. I think Bevoir had been supplyin' 'em with liquor."

"His old trick," murmured Dave. "And it always works—with such Indians as he gets to aid him in his dirty work."

The matter was talked over, and James Morris said he would take a look at the enemy himself. Dave begged to be taken along, and his parent consented.

It was an easy matter to follow the trail Tony Jadwin had made. Walking through the snow, they made no noise, and soon reached the point of vantage the old trapper had occupied. They found the enemy encamped in the midst of a patch of wood, with some rocks on one side. Stationing themselves behind the rocks they readily saw and heard a good deal of what occurred.

The four Frenchmen spoke in French, while the Indians used their native language. As a consequence, Dave understood but little of what was said. But Mr. Morris could speak French fairly well, and understood much of the red men's dialect. He took in every word that reached his ears, and as he listened his brow darkened.

At the end of an hour the talk came to an end, and Indians and French got ready to move. There were four horses in the camp, which Jean Bevoir and his countrymen rode, leaving the Indians to accompany them on foot. Bevoir was scarred from his wounds, and limped as he mounted his steed.

"I ought to put a bullet through that rascal's head!" whispered James Morris. "He is not worthy to live."

"If they discover us they will surely kill us, father," whispered Dave, in return. "They can easily track us through the snow. Even as it is, they may come across our tracks and follow us up."

"I know it, Dave—and I shall do nothing now."

The enemy were soon on their way, following what was a trail leading to the far west. James Morris saw them depart with a darker look than ever on his face.

"The rascals! The infamous scoundrels!" he cried, when he dared to speak in louder tones.

"What did you learn, father?" asked the son.

"A great deal, Dave. Do you know what Jean Bevoir intends to do?"

"I haven't the least idea."

"He and his followers, including that Benoit Vascal, are going to join forces with a large body of Indians. They are going to induce other Frenchmen to do likewise, if they can. The Indians are to aid the Frenchmen in an attack on every trading post for miles around, and whenever successful French and Indians are to divide the plunder."

"Well, they have done just as bad things before."

"That is not all. If the other Indians are finally subdued Jean Bevoir is to take charge of my old trading post, producing a paper to the effect that I once signed over all my rights to the place to him. To this document the other Frenchmen will affix their names as witnesses."

"Oh, what a rascally thing to do!"

"In return for aiding Jean Bevoir, Benoit Vascal is also to receive favors," went on James Morris. "Do you remember the papers that were lost—those relating to Mr. Maurice Hamilton's right to certain tracts of land along the St. Lawrence?"

"Of course."

"Well, Vascal will have duplicates made and have the rights transferred to himself, the others being witnesses to this instrument. Thus, they will cheat the father of the twins out of his property."

"But what will they do when you turn up, and when Mr. Hamilton appears?"

"That is the most dastardly part of the whole business. They are either going to poison us in secret or else capture us and turn us over to some Indians, who, for a consideration, will make way with us in such a fashion that the authorities will be completely baffled."

"How awful, father! How can a man like Jean Bevoir be so bloodthirsty?"

"It is his old hatred of me grown more bitter day by day. He hated me when first we established rival trading posts, and now he cannot bear to think of the English winning this war against the French and Indians and see me getting what is justly my due."

"And what do you intend to do about it?"

"I do not know yet—I must think the matter over, and perhaps I will consult with Captain Ecuyer and Colonel Bouquet. They certainly ought to know about such dastardly plots as these."

Mr. Morris and Dave rejoined the others, and there told of what had been heard. Peaceful Jones, who was in reality a most pugnacious trapper, wanted to attack the enemy on the spot.

"We kin mow 'em all down afore they know what's struck 'em," said he. "Come on in an' have a shindy!"

"I will not risk it—it is asking too much of you," answered James Morris. "Were it necessary it would be different. Let them escape for the time being. Another time we may be better able to cope with them."

From a safe distance they saw the Frenchmen and the Indians move along the trail they had chosen. Soon the coming of night hid them from view. Dave drew a sigh of relief.

"I wish we could get rid of Jean Bevoir," he said. "He has caused us so much trouble."

"There is one comfort," said his father, with a faint smile. "'Forewarned is forearmed.' I know what he intends to do, and I can accordingly lay my plans to thwart him."

"Do you think the French government will allow such actions?"

"Scarcely, Dave—yet, as matters stand to-day, he may be able to explain matters to their satisfaction. Remember, at the present time all Frenchmen are very bitter against the English."

"I wish we could capture that Benoit Vascal. I am certain he can tell us a good deal more about the twins, if he will only open his mouth."

"Vascal and Bevoir seem to be tarred with the same stick. Both are rascals and will do anything to get hold of money. I am afraid we shall have a great deal of trouble before we have seen the last of them," concluded James Morris, and his forecast was correct, as later events amply proved.

CHAPTER XIV
A FIGHT WITH A WOLVERINE

The whole party had lost much of their interest in the hunt, and it was decided to return to Fort Pitt without delay. They went into camp for the night at the spot the enemy had occupied.

"It is going to be cold to-night," said Tony Jadwin, and his words proved true. A keen, penetrating wind started up, and they were glad enough to crouch as close to the fire as possible.

After an early breakfast they started for the fort by another trail. On this they were fortunate enough to come across three deer, caught in something of a hollow between the rocks. Henry brought one of the animals down and the frontiersmen shot the others. Later on Dave got a shot at some partridges and brought down two that were plump and tender.

"Well, we shall not go back empty-handed," said James Morris.

When they reached the fort they found the garrison on strict guard duty. A report had come in from the northward that some of the Six Nations were not going to agree on peace, but were marching to reduce the stronghold. The report was false, but it kept those at Fort Pitt on the watch for a week.

Captain Ecuyer listened to James Morris's story with interest, and when Colonel Bouquet came in he did the same.

"I do not see what can be done at present," said the commandant of the fort. "I cannot send any men out to your trading post this winter. It may be that we can do something in the spring."

This was what Colonel Bouquet said also, and the trader had to accept it as final. But the delay chafed him.

"I have an idea of making my way to the post," said he to his son. "I know it will not be a very nice trip at this time of year, but I would like to arrive there before Jean Bevoir has a chance to settle down and make himself at home."

"If you go of course you will take me along," returned Dave, instantly.

"No, I was thinking of taking only two or three of the old trappers. You see, if we cannot get into the post we shall have to stay in the forest and get our living as best we can, and that will be hard,—if the winter proves a severe one."

The matter was talked over for a week, but nothing came of it just then. But at the end of the next week James Morris arranged to go west, taking Tony Jadwin, Peaceful Jones, and a trapper named Pomeroy with him. They elected to go on foot, taking some snowshoes with them. Each was to carry a good stock of provisions and also plenty of ammunition.

"If we get into the post and have no further trouble, I will send Pomeroy back with the news and also with a letter of instructions," said James Morris.

"And supposing you can't get into the post?" said Dave.

"Then we may stay in that vicinity, or we may come back—just as I think best."

"But you will send some kind of word, won't you?" inquired Henry.

"Yes, I will send word of some kind before the New Year," answered his uncle.

The two youths saw the expedition well on its way, going out with it a distance of three miles. Then came an affectionate parting, and those moving to the west were lost to view down the snowy forest trail.

"I wish I was going along," said Dave, with a deep sigh.

"The same here, Dave," answered his cousin. "But your father did not wish it, and so we shall have to stay at the fort. I hope all goes well with them."

"Yes, I shouldn't wish father to fall into the clutches of Jean Bevoir. Oh, how I despise that rascal!"

The youths had decided to try a bit of hunting while they were out. Henry led the way into the forest, and they wandered along until they came to the tracks of some wild animal.

"What is it?" asked Dave.

"It stumps me," answered his cousin. "It is certain not the track of a deer."

"Maybe it's a bear, or a buffalo."

"I don't think so. But whatever it is, it was carrying something in its mouth."

"How do you know that?"

"Don't you see the occasional dip in the snow alongside of the trail? The load was heavy and sagged down at times."

"Shall we follow the trail up?"

"I'm willing."

The trail led into the very depths of the great forest, and to help them from getting lost they broke off the bushes here and there, thus "blazing" the trail as they proceeded. In the open spaces the wind had drifted the snow quite a little, but where the trail led the walking proved fairly easy.

"The animal certainly traveled a good distance," remarked Dave, after almost a mile had been covered.

"We are coming to the end now," answered Henry, whose keen eyes took in every detail of the trail.

"How do you know that?"

"Don't you see how the dips increase? That shows the load was growing heavier. The steps are shorter too."

"Henry, it's wonderful how you notice such things!"

"Not at all. I only keep my eyes open, that's all. Now we had better keep quiet, or we may scare the game away."

After that they proceeded a short distance further. Then they reached a clearing, where the heavy wind of the summer previous had cut down several of the tallest trees.

"There must have been a whirlwind here," whispered Dave.

"Hush, the trail leads under that mass of piled-up trees," returned Henry. "Got your gun ready?"

"Yes."

Dave had hardly spoken when there came a snarl from under the mass of trees, and looking down both young hunters saw a pair of gleaming eyes glaring hatefully at them.

"It's a bear!" cried Dave.

"No, a wolverine!" burst out Henry. "And an ugly one, too. Look out for yourself."

Henry was indeed right; it was a wolverine they had trailed to its lair—a ferocious beast, sometimes known as a glutton, because of its enormous appetite for meat. The wolverine was of unusual size, with a shaggy body of brownish-black. The muzzle was darker than the rest of the beast, and under the throat were several whitish spots. The upper lip hairs were long and coarse, and the fangs keener than those of a wolf.

The wolverine had been feasting on the carcass of a fox, but the meal had evidently not sweetened his temper. Suddenly he turned and disappeared from view along the tree-branches.

"He has gone," said Dave.

"Keep your eyes open!" shouted Henry. "He means fight! I know the kind!"

A moment passed and the wolverine reappeared, this time on an upper limb of a fallen tree. He gave one low snarl and then sprang directly for Dave's throat.

Crack! It was Henry's rifle that spoke up. The aim was a hasty one, and the wolverine was hit in the hind quarters. Dave slipped to one side, and the beast landed at his feet. Then Dave stepped back, to get a shot, but the beast whirled around in the snow and once more gained the shelter of his lair.

The two young hunters lost no time in retreating, but Henry kept Dave from going too close to any bushes in the vicinity.

"You can't trust a wolverine," he said. "Load up quick—and keep your eyes wide open. He may be at our backs next."

Dave was well aware of their danger. He had heard of a hunter being killed by a wolverine and heard Sam Barringford say that the beast was the most treacherous of animals. If cornered a wolverine will often fight to the death, no matter what the odds. It has been known to attack animals much larger than itself.

The two young hunters reloaded with speed and kept their eyes on the fallen trees. They saw a branch move, but could not see the wolverine. Dave, it must be confessed, began to grow a trifle nervous.

"Do you see him?" he asked, after fully a minute had passed.

"No, but—— There he is! Look out!"

The wolverine had appeared on one of the highest of the tree-branches. He made a lightning-like leap and gained one of the neighboring trees. Dave took a quick shot, but missed his mark. Then the body of the wolverine was hidden by the broad tree-limb.

"Let us get out of this," said Dave. "Before we know it, one of us will get hurt."

"I am going to kill that wolverine," answered Henry, determinedly, all his hunting instinct on edge over what had already occurred.

"What's the use? He is no good for meat."

"The beast is not going to get the better of me."

Henry walked around the tree with care. He got a slight glimpse of the wolverine's bushy tail, but that was all.

"Can you see him, Henry?"

"I know where he is. I think I can make him move."

Henry picked up some snow, made a snowball, and threw it at the bushy tail. There was a snarl and a snap, and down into the snow leaped the wolverine, all ready for a fight.

As soon as the beast landed Dave fired. As luck would have it, the wolverine was hit in the side and turned over and over, sending the snow in all directions.

"I've got him! I've got him!" called out the young hunter, excitedly.

"I reckon I'd better finish him," answered Henry, and once again his rifle spoke up. At once the whirling of the wolverine ceased, and he stretched himself out on the snow.

"My gracious! that was a fight," observed Dave, wiping the cold perspiration from his forehead. "I don't wonder some folks think there is nothing so savage as a wolverine."

"We want to be on guard still," said Henry. "Load up. His mate may be around here, and they say a she-wolverine is ten times worse than a he-one."

"She'll certainly be bad enough when she learns that we have killed her mate."

"We may as well give up hunting around here," went on Henry. "Our shots have probably scared away any deer that may be in this vicinity."

"We can look for small game, Henry. I don't want to go back empty-handed."

"Listen!"

The two young hunters were reloading, when Henry uttered the exclamation.

"What did you hear?" asked Dave.

"Sounded to me like a wolf, and it was pretty close too."

"I hope we don't meet any wolves in this forest!" cried Dave.

Both listened, and soon heard three more wolves. They were coming along the trail made by the wolverine and the youths.

"I see them! And they are coming directly for us!" cried Dave, a minute later, and as he spoke eight or nine wolves burst into view, coming forward on a run, their eyes gleaming and their fangs showing viciously.

CHAPTER XV
WOLVES, AND A SNOWSTORM

The two young hunters knew from former experience that it would be useless to attempt to shoot down so many wolves, and so they looked around for some other means whereby to escape from the beasts, who were evidently hungry and bloodthirsty.

"Into one of the trees!" cried Henry, and slung his rifle over his shoulder. His cousin did likewise, and both caught hold of some tree-limbs just as the wolves drew near. One made a snap at them, but they managed to get out of the reach of the animal before any damage was done.

As was to be expected, the first wolves to appear were the forerunners of a pack, and soon, to the consternation of Dave and Henry, more of the beasts appeared until they could count forty. They snapped and snarled, and several fell upon the carcass of the wolverine and tore it into pieces.

"That's the way they'd like to tear us into bits," remarked Dave, with a shudder over the sight.

"Dave, no two ways about it, we are in a pickle."

"And likely to stay there for some time to come, Henry."

"That's the truth of it. Trying to shoot such a pack is utterly impossible."

"And I doubt if we can drive 'em away either."

Just to try the effects of a shot, both took careful aim, each at a big wolf. The beasts went down, one killed outright and the other mortally wounded. The rest of the pack retreated for a few minutes, then came forward as before.

"See, they are eating up the dead one!" said Henry, and it was true. The carcass was hauled and pulled and torn apart, the wolves fighting greedily over the pieces. The wounded wolf crawled off in the snow and later followed the fate of the other.

After firing the two shots the young hunters reloaded as before and sat down among the tree-branches to consider the situation. It was about noon, and both were hungry.

"We are fortunate in having some rations along," remarked Dave. "But it will be dry eating, without a drink of water."

However, they ate their meal, taking their time, as there seemed nothing else to do. In the meantime, the wolves sat around the tree in a wide circle, watching them intently. There would be a spell of silence, then one of the number would growl or snap and in a moment the whole pack would be at it. Then another silence would follow.

"This is certainly growing interesting," observed Dave, as he swallowed the last of his food. "I'd give a sixpence for a drink of water."

"And two shillings to have the wolves go away," added Henry, with a grin. "Dave, perhaps we are booked to stay here all night."

"It will be a cold roosting-place. As it is I am pretty cold."

To keep warm they slapped their arms across their chests, and hammered their heels against the tree-trunk. In doing this Dave suddenly slipped and fell.

"Look out!" cried his cousin, and made a clutch at him. Both went down, one on one side of a limb and one on the other. Henry had Dave by the arm, and there they hung for a moment, with the wolves below, leaping up and snapping as never before.

"Don't let go!" shrieked Dave, who had no desire to fall among those snapping jaws waiting to receive him.

Henry clung fast, although it was no easy matter to sustain his cousin in such an unusual position. His wrist was twisted painfully. Then each caught the limb with his free hand, and they both swung up to safety once more.

"That was a narrow squeak!" gasped Dave. "I thought the wolves had me sure. I hope you didn't get hurt, Henry."

"Got my wrist scraped a little, that's all," was the reply. "But please don't slip down again. Where's your gun?"

Dave felt around in dismay. Then he looked below. The strap had broken and the weapon lay in the snow among the wolves.

"You'll not do any more shooting just yet," went on Henry, grimly.

"It's too bad!" cried Dave. "The strap wasn't very good, but I thought it would hold for this trip. Look out that yours doesn't drop, Henry."

"I'll try to keep it on hand."

Once again there came a period of waiting. So far it had been clear, but now it commenced to cloud over.

"We are going to have either snow or rain," announced Dave.

"Well, of the two I hope it is snow," said Henry. "I don't want to get wet through in such cold weather as this. It will give us our death of cold."

A little while after that it began to snow. At first the flakes were large and drifted down like so many feathers. But soon they grew smaller and came down so thickly that a large portion of the landscape was blotted out. Then a wind sprung up, making the situation of the young hunters anything but comfortable.

"The wolves are leaving!" cried Henry, presently, as an extra blast of wind sent the snow swirling around. "They don't like this storm. Reckon they are afraid of being snowed in."

"I don't like the storm myself," returned his cousin. "See how thickly the snow is coming down now."

Soon the last of the wolves had disappeared and silence reigned in that part of the vast forest. With caution they let themselves down to the ground, and Dave picked up his gun, cleaned it, and put on a new priming.

"We'll have to watch out for those wolves," he cautioned.

"If they come for us, we can climb another tree," answered Henry. "But I don't think they will turn back. Their lair may be miles from here, and they will want to get there before they become snowbound."

The falling snow had covered the wolverine trail, and it was with difficulty that they could see the bushes they had broken off while journeying along. It was growing darker and the snow swirled and blew in every direction, almost blinding them.

"This will delay father," observed Dave. "The party will have to go into camp and stay there until the storm clears away."

"We may have to go into camp ourselves, Dave."

"Perhaps so. This puts me in mind of the time Sam Barringford and I were journeying to Fort Oswego, and got caught in a terrible storm—the time we got a bear."

"You were after Jean Bevoir then, weren't you?"

"Yes, we thought he had Nell as a prisoner. My, but that was a howler, Henry!"

"Well, this is going to be a howler, too! Listen to the wind rising!"

There was no need to listen, for they could not have shut out the sound had they tried. The flakes of snow had given way to fine, hard particles resembling salt, and these pelted them in the face until they could not see and had to turn around to catch their breath.

"May as well give it up," said Henry, after struggling along for almost a mile. "Let us find some place under the cedars."

They had reached a spot where the cedars were plentiful, and picked out one with the lower boughs bent down to the ground. Getting under this they were sheltered from the biting wind, and had a chance to rest and consider the situation.

"One thing is certain, I don't want to stay out all night without something to eat and without a fire," said Henry, who loved all the comforts of a hunter's life. "We must find a better shelter than this. We can't start a blaze here without the danger of setting fire to the forest."

"I'm willing to go anywhere, providing it isn't too far," answered Dave.

Having rested for half an hour they started onward once more. They soon reached a spot that looked familiar to both of them.

"Hurrah! I know where we are now!" cried Dave.

"So do I, and I know where we can find a pretty good shelter," added Henry.

He referred to what had once been an Indian village, long before the French and English had come to that territory. Here, among the ruins, was located an old council-house, of logs and bark, with a sort of fireplace at one end.

"At the old Indian village?"

"Yes."

They hurried on, for it was now growing night. Both had their guns over their backs, but presently Henry swung his weapon around to the front.

"Maybe we'll be able to pick up something for supper and breakfast," he observed.

It did not take long to reach the deserted village. Nothing was standing but the old council-house, and that was next to being a wreck. As they stepped over the threshold they saw something hop away through an open doorway on the other side. Quickly Henry blazed away.

"A rabbit, and a fat one too!" he cried, holding up the game. "That is better than nothing."

They stirred around and soon found a nest of the animals and killed two more. Then they put down their guns and went out to find some firewood. It was cold work, and they were half frozen by the time they had a blaze started. They piled on several big sticks of wood and soon began to warm up.

"This is not so bad but that it might be worse," declared Dave, while they were preparing one of the rabbits for supper.

Searching around they came across a small iron pot. It was rusty, but they managed to scour it out, and then melted some snow for drinking water. One rabbit tasted so good that they cooked a second, for the walk and the keen air had made them tremendously hungry. They took their time over the meal, for they had nothing else to do.

"I think I'll try to close up some of the openings," remarked Henry, after they had finished picking the bones. "We can do it with cedar branches."

With their hunting knives they cut a quantity of cedar branches and placed them in the broken-out doors and windows of the old council-house. This kept out most of the wind, and soon the temperature rose so that it was far more comfortable within than before. Then they brought in some more wood for the fire, that the blaze might last through the night.

"I suppose this was a well-known place at one time," observed Dave, as he gazed around the structure. "What famous addresses the Indian chiefs must have delivered here!"

"Yes, and what plans they laid to massacre the whites," replied Henry. "If these walls could talk they could tell some cruel stories, I'm thinking."

"Henry, I don't think the Indians are altogether to blame."

"Why not?"

"Because they haven't been treated just right, that's why. The land used to belong to them."

"Humph! They never tilled it, did they? They can't expect to let this fine soil lie in idleness for century after century."

"But they had rights which neither the French nor the English have respected."

"Do you stick up for such a wily wretch as Pontiac?"

"No, but I stick up for such a noble red man as White Buffalo."

"Oh, well, if they were all like White Buffalo there wouldn't be any trouble."

They sat by the fire a good hour, talking about the Indians, the departure of James Morris for the trading post, and about the folks at home and other matters. Then they grew sleepy, and lay down to rest, never realizing the double peril so close at hand.

CHAPTER XVI
SAVED BY A WINDSTORM

The two young hunters had been asleep perhaps ten minutes when a form stole forward from behind a corner post in the old council-house.

The form was that of a young Seneca warrior, Boka the Fox, a red man known for miles around for his skill in hunting and fishing. No matter who went out with him Boka the Fox usually got the biggest turkey, the biggest deer, and very often the biggest fish.

Boka the Fox was alone. He had been spying in the vicinity of Fort Pitt, and was now on his way westward to report what he had seen. The storm had overtaken him, and fancy had caused him to seek shelter in the deserted village. He had come up just at the arrival of Dave and Henry and had heard the gunshots when the rabbits were brought down.

Despite the snowstorm, Boka the Fox waited around patiently for some chance to do the whites an injury. He had only his hunting knife with him— a weapon taken from a murdered frontiersman some months before. His bow had been broken the day before and his tomahawk had been lost during a wild flight to get away from some soldiers who had seen him on the trail and fired several shots after his retreating form.

Not to remain out in the howling storm—for the wind was growing wilder every moment—Boka the Fox had wormed his way into a small recess close to the rude fireplace of which this council-house boasted. I say boasted, for the majority of such places had only an open place where a fire might be built, the smoke rising directly to the outer air.

In his warm corner the red warrior waited patiently for Dave and Henry to go to sleep. Several times he was in danger of being discovered, and he kept his hand on the handle of his knife, ready to battle the instant he was seen. He heard every word that was spoken, but understood only a little.

The wind was now whistling shrilly around the old council-house, causing the dilapidated building to creak and groan and quiver from end to end. With so much noise, Boka the Fox stepped forward boldly to the center of the room. The fire was still bright, and he could distinctly see the faces of the two youths as they slept.

"Boka must kill both before either awakens," murmured the Indian.

"Boka must kill both before either awakens," murmured the Indian in his native tongue. "Then he can take their guns and all of their belongings and fly as soon as the storm ceases."

He dropped the blanket he had been wearing, so that he might be free to act, and draw himself up, knife in hand,—a tall, slim figure, with a face full of shrewdness and treachery.

As he took a step towards Dave the wind came up once more, shaking the old building worse than ever. Henry turned uneasily in his sleep, and gave a deep sigh. The Indian turned toward the youth, thinking to kill him before he had a chance to rouse up.

There was now a sudden spell of silence—so unusual and so impressive that the Indian was compelled to stop in his dastardly work and listen. It was as if the wind had ceased utterly.

Then, with almost the quickness of lightning, came a strange humming sound, accompanied by the cracking of trees and tree-limbs, and the fierce pelting of hard snow as it swept along on the wings of a tornado. The onrush of the elements was directly for the old council-house, and in a twinkling the building was caught up and fairly blown into the air.

"Henry!" gasped Dave, as he found himself rolled over and over in the snow. "What in the world is this?"

There was no answer—indeed, no answer could have been heard above that terrible shrieking and humming of the wind. In the path of the tornado the trees were being mowed down from one end of the forest to the other. Branches were flying in all directions, and when Dave tried to rise he found himself powerless to do so. He was rolled over and over again, and at last brought up against a tree-stump, out of breath and completely bewildered.

Inside of five minutes the tornado was a thing of the past and the wind died down to a moderate breeze. The fire that had been built in the old council-house had been blown in a heap between two old tree-stumps and was still blazing away, thus affording some light. Where the two youths had been sleeping were half a dozen broken and twisted tree-limbs, partly covered with snow.

It took Dave some little time to recover his breath. He had to feel of himself, to make sure that no limbs were broken. He looked around for Henry, but his cousin was nowhere in sight.

"Henry!" he called, loudly. "Where are you? Henry!"

He repeated the cry many times, walking slowly around the wreck of the council-house and among the trees which had been blown down in that vicinity. At last came a faint response, and running in the direction of the sound he found poor Henry wedged under some heavy tree-branches.

"Tak—take them off!" gasped the prisoner. "I—I can hardly breathe."

To remove the big limbs was impossible, but after a good deal of maneuvering, Dave managed to raise one branch a little and Henry crawled through the snow from underneath. Then he sat on the branch panting for breath.

"It's a windstorm," said Dave. "About the worst I ever saw."

"Whe—where is the house?"

"Gone—the wind took it up like a kite. Henry, we can be thankful that we weren't killed."

"You are right. Oh, how my breast hurts!"

"Any ribs broken, do you think?"

"No, I think I—I am scraped more than anything else," answered the injured one.

As the fire was in a safe place, Dave stirred it up and helped Henry to a spot where he might keep warm. Then Dave dragged some tree-branches up in a semicircle, to keep off what little was left of the wind.

"We'll have to look for our guns and traps," said Henry. "Have you any idea where they are?"

"They can't be far off, Henry. But why not wait until morning?"

"It's not safe. Some wild animal might attack us."

Taking a firebrand Dave made a torch of it and began a hunt. Soon he came across Henry's rifle and other things. Then he brought out of the snow a hunting knife.

"Hullo! Whose hunting knife is this?" he asked, examining it carefully. "Henry, you didn't have this, did you?"

"I did not," was the answer. "I never saw it before. Let me see. It's got the initials R. D. C. on it. I don't know anybody by those letters, do you?"

"Old Dick Capenfeld. He was killed by the Indians several weeks ago."

"I'd like to know how the knife got here."

The young hunters looked the blade over, and then both sat down by the fire. Presently Henry feel asleep once more, and after a bit Dave followed his example.

When they awoke it was dawn, and the storm had cleared away completely. The fire had died down, but it was easily replenished, and then both of the youths began a systematic hunt for the rest of their belongings. Henry declared that he felt all right, saving for a certain stiffness across the chest, where the tree-limb had held him down.

Dave was stirring among some heavy tree-branches when he leaped back with a loud cry.

"An Indian!"

"An Indian! Where?" came from Henry, and he caught up his rifle.

"Here—between the tree-limbs. I—I reckon he is dead."

Henry ran to the spot, and both of the young hunters gazed at Boka the Fox. The tornado had caught up the Indian and landed him head first in the branches of a tree laid low by the mighty wind. In turning over the red warrior had been unable to save himself, and his neck had been broken, killing him instantly.

"This beats the kingdom!" cried Dave. "Henry, that Indian must have been on hand when the tornado occurred!"

"Like as not he was watching us."

"And maybe he was going to kill us."

"The finding of that hunting knife makes it look that way, Dave."

"Perhaps there are more near by."

The two young hunters looked around without delay—Henry holding his rifle ready for use, should a warrior appear. They were greatly upset and did not quiet down for half an hour.

"He must have been alone," said Henry, at last. "Where he came from there is no telling. Well, if he was going to kill us, it was a lucky thing that the tornado came along as it did and stopped him."

They continued their search in the snow and among the fallen trees, and presently uncovered Dave's rifle and the rest of the traps, and also the last of the rabbits. This they spitted over the fire and ate for breakfast.

"Now we may as well get back to the fort—before another storm overtakes us," said Henry.

"What about the Indian?"

"Leave him where he is. I reckon the wolves will take care of him. I am not going to bother myself on his account."

"I hope the tornado didn't overtake father and his party," went on Dave. "It's a wonder we weren't killed."

"Yes, we can certainly be thankful,—not only because we escaped from the windstorm, but for escaping from that Indian."

The wind had swept the snow into great drifts or ridges, and they knew they would have to make wide detours in order to escape the worst of these piles. They kicked out the fire, picked up their traps and the blanket of the dead Indian, and set out.

It was a hard, exhausting journey, and they often stopped to rest. On their way they saw in the distance a small deer, stalled in a snowdrift, and Henry could not resist the temptation to fire. The deer leaped into the air, threw up a flurry of snow, and then disappeared from view.

"There's something to take to the fort!" cried the young hunter.

"It will be all we can carry," observed Dave.

"What! you wouldn't leave a deer behind, would you?" questioned Henry, reproachfully.

"Oh, no."

With care they worked their way around to where the deer had disappeared in the snow. To do this they had to cross a hollow, where they sank up to their waists.

"Look out, or you'll get stuck!" sang out Dave, and just then Henry sank to his armpits. He floundered around a good deal before he emerged from the hollow, blowing like a winded ox.

The deer had fallen over a small cliff, and they had something of a task raising it up. But at last they had the game secure, and they carried it between them, slung on a long, slender pole.

"Hurrah! I see the fort!" cried Dave, an hour later, as they drew to the top of a long hill. "The worst of the trip is over."

He was right, and by noon they reached Fort Pitt. They were glad to rest and eat a hearty dinner, after which they told their story. The effects of the windstorm had been felt at the fort, but no great damage had been done.

CHAPTER XVII
THE JOURNEY TO THE TRADING POST

Leaving Dave and Henry at Fort Pitt, let us shift the scene further westward and note how James Morris and his party fared on their way towards the trading post on the Ohio River.

The party felt the full effects of the snowstorm, and had to go into a temporary camp. The wind, however, hardly touched them, and they were left in ignorance of the great damage done in other directions.

"'Tis lucky we brought our snowshoes with us," said Peaceful Jones. "With such a fall, most of our traveling will have to be with the shoes on."

They had gone into camp under some overhanging rocks, where a big fire had kept them warm. The old trappers had brought down a deer and some rabbits, so they did not suffer for the want of food, having brought along two slabs of bacon, some beans and flour, and likewise a few cooking utensils.

On the morning after the snowstorm they set off early, and by the middle of the afternoon found themselves ten miles further on their journey in the direction of the post. It had been hard work to travel on the snowshoes, over a trail which was all but obliterated, and Pomeroy requested that they rest again.

"I've been a-loafin' around thet fort so much I ain't got my walkin' legs yit," was the manner in which he expressed himself. "Maybe I'll hev 'em by ter-morrer."

"I fancy we all need the rest," answered James Morris. "I am stiff myself. We'll get used to the snowshoes in a day or two."

They searched for another resting-place, and James Morris found a spot he had used for that purpose when he had first gone west—to establish himself on the Kinotah.

"That seems a long time ago," said the trader, to Tony Jadwin. "And think of all that has happened since! The war with France, and the capture of Fort Pitt, Niagara, Quebec, Montreal, and a number of other places, and then this war with Pontiac and the tribes under him. Surely, Tony, we can be thankful that we live to tell about it."

"Yes," answered the trapper addressed. "And think of the fights at the old trading post and then at the new one! And we ain't done yet, I am sorry to say."

"Sometimes I wonder if it is worth all the trouble and risk", continued James Morris. "I have gained a little, but it has cost me dear."

"I'd never give in to the Indians or to them Frenchmen, Mr. Morris. Why, if you give 'em a pound they'll want a thousand."

"I know that."

"The land in the west belongs to the English now, and a fair share of it is yours. Those Indians and those Frenchmen have got to leave us alone, an' the sooner they learn the lesson the better," concluded Tony Jadwin.

The new resting-place was where some tall trees grew on the very edge of a cliff. One tree had fallen, and its gigantic roots hung over the cliff, forming a network over which it was easy to place some pine branches. As the cliff was hollowed out just beyond the trees, this left a space about eight feet deep by twenty feet long where they could make themselves comfortable. Against the rocks they built a fire, the smoke escaping through some crevices. They cooked themselves a haunch of venison and some beans and biscuits, and took their own time about eating. All went to sleep as soon as it grew dark, knowing that a long, hard tramp lay before them at daybreak.

The travelers were destined not to be allowed to rest undisturbed. James Morris slept several hours when he was awakened by having a cold nose pressed against his face. He opened his eyes and sat up and at the same instant heard a low growl.

"A bear!" he yelled, as loudly as he could. "A bear! Two of them!"

The trader was right—two full-grown bears had entered the camp, evidently attracted by the smell of venison and bacon. As James Morris arose the bears retreated to another part of the shelter, one stepping directly upon Peaceful Jones.

"Git orf o' me, ye sinner!" gasped the frontiersman, wrathfully. "Git orf, I say!" And then as the bear backed away, he reached for his rifle and tried to take aim. But Mr. Morris was in the way, and he did not dare to pull the trigger.

By this time the whole camp was in an uproar. Tony Jadwin tried to rise, but just as he did so one of the bears ran against him, pitching him down in such a fashion that one hand went into the smoldering fire.

"Great hamstrings!" roared the trapper, wiping the hot ashes from his hand. "What's this mean? Two b'ars, eh? Shoot 'em, somebody! Shoot em!"

The bears were now evidently as much frightened as those who had been asleep, and tumbling against the rocks and the tree-roots they got out of the shelter and ran off along a stretch which the wind had swept clear of snow.

The commotion made some dirt and snow fall on the fire, practically extinguishing it.

"Stir up that fire, Pomeroy," said James Morris, as soon as something like quietness had been restored. The man addressed did so and piled on some light brushwood, so that they might look around them. They found much in disorder, and soon made the discovery that the bears had carried off every pound of the meat.

"They didn't do it just now," said Tony Jadwin. "They must have made two trips o' it. Likely they didn't get enough the first time. Drat the luck, anyway! We kin shoot some more venison, but we can't git no bacon, an' bacon is what I like best." In those days deer meat was so plentiful among the hunters that many grew tired of eating it, just as many farmers to-day get tired of eating chickens.

Had it been daylight some of the party would have been in favor of following the bears up and shooting them. But this was voted out of the question in the darkness, and so they retired once more, leaving one man, however, to remain on guard and attend to the fire.

The next day the weather remained clear and the sun made the snow pack down a trifle, so that it became easier to walk on snowshoes. The route lay over several hills and then along a frozen watercourse where the ice was as smooth as glass.

"You want to be careful here", observed Pomeroy. "This ice ain't so hard as it looks. We ain't had much winter, outside o' the snowstorm."

They followed the stream until they came to a bend, and then started to cross over. Tony Jadwin was in advance, when he heard a shout from Peaceful Jones.

"A deer!"

All looked and saw the deer, but a long distance off. Anxious to get a shot, Peaceful Jones started along the river bank on the icy snow. He had gone only a few steps, when they suddenly saw him throw up his hands and disappear from view.

"Hello! What does that mean?" exclaimed James Morris. "Was he shot?"

"Either thet or he went through a hole," answered one of the other men.

All brought their rifles around, ready for use, and then started toward the spot where the trapper had disappeared so suddenly. They saw a hole in the snow.

"He is down there!" cried James Morris. "Come, we must get him out."

"I think we had better take turns watching," said Henry.

This was easier said than done. The hole was ten or twelve feet deep. The men on the surface of the snow joined hands, and thus held James Morris from falling in as the trader bent over the hole. Looking down, he could see Jones below, spluttering wildly.

"Sa—sa—save me!" were his first words. The man was so chilled that he could do scarcely more than chatter.

"We will," answered James Morris.

He directed the last man on the line to pass forward a rifle, and he took hold of the barrel of this, while he allowed Peaceful Jones to grasp the stock. Then James Morris began to pull, and Peaceful Jones came up, over the edge of the hole, and was quickly drawn to a place of safety.

The man was so chilled that the others lost no time in building a big fire, in the meantime covering him with a blanket. Then, while he was getting warm, Pomeroy went fishing with a stick and some lines, and after a lot of trouble succeeded in bringing up Jones's rifle.

"I was a-lookin' at the deer, an' didn't see the hole," was the explanation the trapper gave of his mishap. "After this I'll look whar I'm steppin'."

"Ye had better," was Pomeroy's comment. "'Cos it might be as thar wouldn't be nobuddy around to help ye out ag'in!"

The river left behind, they passed on directly to the region where the first trading post had been located. This was still suffering from the effects of the burn-over, although here and there a few trees and bushes had sprouted out during the past summer.

"It was a fine spot," said James Morris, as he stood and surveyed the site of the old post. "A fine spot. But it is no good now, and will not be for years to come."

"As good as it was, the site of the new post is better," answered Tony Jadwin. "In fact, I think that the new spot is the finest in this section of the country."

"And I suppose that is why Jean Bevoir wishes to get possession of it," went on the trader, with a trace of bitterness in his tones.

"Jean Bevoir knows a good thing when he sees it," said Peaceful Jones. "He's about ez wise ez he is wicked."

"I think his party must have passed this way," put in Pomeroy, who had been walking around. "Thar's been a camp in yonder trees not long ago—I kin tell it by the fresh-burnt sticks."

"Perhaps some Indians have been here," said James Morris. "Bevoir and his followers must have reached the trading post long ago."

"Not if they were stopped on the way."

At this remark a sudden hope sprang into the breast of the trader.

"It would be a fine thing if he had been stopped and we could get there first!" he cried. "But I am afraid that is hoping for too much. However, let us not linger here, but move forward at once."

The others were willing, and without delay the journey down to the Ohio was resumed. Every foot of the way was familiar to all of the party, and one or the other took the lead, over trails which their feet had trod in times of war as well as in peace.

"The Ohio at last!" said James Morris, at noon of the next day. "I am glad to see this broad stream once more."

They were now within a few miles of the trading post, and all hurried forward with much interest, curious to learn what they should find when they arrived there.

CHAPTER XVIII
RUNNING INTO A TRAP

"There is the post!"

It was James Morris who said this. He was slightly in advance of the others, and coming around a bend of the Ohio River caught sight of the place which had cost him so much hard work to establish.

As my old readers know, the trading post proper was a substantial building of heavy logs, containing four rooms, the main one of which was usually devoted to trading with the trappers and Indians. Near by was a storehouse of two rooms, with a stable attached for horses and cattle.

The site of the trading post was a small bluff fronting the broad Ohio, and not far away was a gurgling brook, with some rough rocks beyond. The buildings and grounds were surrounded by a strong palisade of sharpened logs, containing, at a convenient point, a gate ten feet in width, locked by two heavy crossbars. The palisade contained many loopholes for shooting purposes in case of attack. Around the outside of the palisade the ground had been cleared for a short distance, but otherwise, excepting for the river, the unbroken forest stretched for many miles. To-day this same locality is dotted with rich farms and villages, with a railroad running through it, and where the canoes of Indians and white hunters used to ride there now plow steamboats and tugboats. And yet this was but a hundred and forty-odd years ago! What wonderful strides our country is making, and who can imagine what the next hundred and forty years will bring forth?

James Morris called a halt, and all gathered around him, wondering what the next move was to be. They looked toward the trading post. The great gate of the palisade was wide open and there appeared to be no sign of life anywhere.

"Looks deserted, don't it?" remarked Tony Jadwin. He had helped to erect the place and knew every nook and corner as well as did its owner.

"It certainly does," answered James Morris. "But we must not take too much for granted."

"'Pears like I kin see tracks in the snow, near the gate," remarked Peaceful Jones. "What do ye think on't, Pomeroy?"

"Some tracks thar certain, but the wind has swept 'em so ye can't tell ef they belong to man or beast."

"Let us walk through the forest and look at the other side of the place," said James Morris, and this was done. Try their best they could see nobody, and from the branches of a tree Tony Jadwin announced that the door to the main building stood wide open.

"Then it's empty," said Pomeroy. "Because, if anybuddy war thar, they'd shet it in sech weather as this."

At last James Morris concluded to venture through the gate, and did so, gun in hand, and followed by the others. A look around the broad grounds revealed nobody, and with a heart that beat strangely, the trader advanced toward the main building.

"Ho! Within there!" he called out, sharply.

He waited, but there was no answer, nor did anybody appear.

"Reckon we've got it all to ourselves," said Pomeroy. "Either Bevoir an' his crowd ain't got here yit, or else they are out on a hunt, or somethin' else."

"I'll soon make sure," said Tony Jadwin, and entered the main building, and James Morris followed him. It was rather dark within, and for the moment they could see next to nothing. Jadwin walked to one side of the room, while the trader stepped to the doorway of the next room. In the meanwhile Pomeroy entered also, leaving only Peaceful Jones outside.

It was then that the scene changed as if by magic. From several places of concealment Jean Bevoir, Benoit Vascal, and a number of Indians under Moon Eye leaped forth and fell upon the three newcomers. James Morris was sent flat on the floor, face downward, so that he could not use his gun, and Tony Jadwin received a blow from a club that stretched him lifeless. Two Indians pounced upon Pomeroy, who uttered a loud cry for assistance. A moment later a tomahawk split Pomeroy's skull in twain, killing him instantly.

Peaceful Jones ran forward and was just in time to see Pomeroy go down, with the hatchet still sticking in his head. He fired at one of the Indians, shooting him through the heart. Then a rifle rang out within the building, and Peaceful Jones felt a bullet graze his shoulder.

"Come on out o' thet!" he roared. "This is too hot fer us!"

"Save yourself!" came faintly from James Morris. "We are trapped! They mean to massacre us!"

His cries were cut short by two pistol shots. Then followed sounds of several blows, and James Morris appeared at the doorway, his face covered with blood. He took one more step forward, and with a gasp sank down in a heap.

From the storehouse now poured half a dozen Indians, armed with bows and arrows and tomahawks. Realizing that it would be useless to fight such a number of the enemy, and satisfied in his own mind that all of his companions were either killed or mortally wounded, Peaceful Jones turned and ran for the rear of the main building. Three arrows whizzed beside him, and a bullet from a pistol flew close to his ear.

"After heem! He must not escape!" came in the voice of Jean Bevoir. "Ve must keel dem all!"

Reaching the back of the main building, Peaceful Jones did not pause. In the snow lay some brushwood, and he caught up a branch of this, and, holding it behind him, continued to run. Two more arrows were sent after him and lodged in the tree-branch, thus saving him from further injury.

As he came close to the corner of the palisade he wondered what he had best do next. The Indians were after him hot-footed and so was one of the Frenchmen. He felt that to make a stand would mean certain death.

He had thus far gained a spot used the year before for sawing and splitting wood. A big saw-buck was still standing there, and he picked it up with ease and continued to run. Reaching the palisade, he stood the saw-buck up on one end and climbed to the top.

"Stop!" roared a voice, in French, and a rifle rang out. The bullet this time struck Peaceful Jones in the left shoulder, inflicting an ugly and painful wound. He gave a grunt, mounted the sharp points of the palisade, and dropped outside. Then, with all the strength that was left to him, he started for the nearest patch of timber, sixty yards distant. As he entered the timber some more arrows flew towards him, but went shy of their mark.

The trapper was now weak from the loss of blood, which was flowing down from his shoulder to his hand. But he staggered on, knowing that he now had no time to stop and bind up his wound. He rushed straight into the forest and staggered onward until he came to a clump of low-branched trees. Then, to "cut the trail," as it was called, he pulled himself up into the trees by his uninjured arm and climbed from one tree to another, and so on, until a hundred feet had been covered. Then he dropped on some rocks, which the wind had swept clear of snow, and went forward as before, gritting his teeth, to keep himself from fainting from loss of blood.

It was well for Peaceful Jones that night was coming on, and in the depths of the forest it was growing dark. Plucky though he was to the last degree, he was but human, and now felt that he might drop from sheer exhaustion at any moment. He looked for some sort of a hiding-place, and reaching a cedar tree growing in a split of the rocks, dove under it.

For a good quarter of an hour the trapper did little but hold his hand tightly over his wound and pant for breath, leaning against the tree in the meanwhile with eyes closed. He could do nothing more to save himself, and was in that condition of mind when capture or escape meant little or nothing to him.

But as his breath came back to him, and none of the Indians or Frenchmen appeared, a spark of hope came to his breast. He tore off his heavy coat and his hunting shirt and examined the wound from which he had suffered the most. The bullet had passed directly through the flesh and some lint was sticking in the wound. He took out the lint, cleaned the wound with soft snow, and bound it up as best he could with a handkerchief and a bandage he carried for emergencies. Then he drew on his hunting shirt once more and his coat, closed his eyes, and fell back in a sort of stupor.

It was pitch-dark when Peaceful Jones came to himself once more. At a distance he heard a murmur of voices. Some Indians and a Frenchman were holding a conversation.

"I can see nothing of a trail," said one of the Indians, in his native tongue. "I doubt if he came this way."

"He must not be allowed to get away," said the Frenchman, also in the Indian tongue. "Dead men are best, since they tell no tales."

"Are the others all dead?" asked another Indian.

"Dead or dying."

"It was lucky that Moon Eye discovered their coming in time," said the first Indian who had spoken. "We set a nice trap for them."

The Indians and the Frenchman continued to talk, in the meantime moving away from the cedar tree, so that Peaceful Jones made out no more of the conversation. He himself could speak the Indian language and understood every word that had been spoken.

The news filled his heart with grief. All his companions were either dead or dying and the enemy were doing their best to find and slay him. He felt that only by the help of Providence would he be enabled to escape. He was not a very religious man, but he breathed a silent prayer to Heaven that he might be spared, if for no other purpose than to carry the sad news back to Fort Pitt.

An hour went by, and the Indians and the Frenchman left the vicinity entirely. But then came something else to disturb and alarm him.

A small bear stepped into view, sniffing the air suspiciously. His den was among the rocks close to the cedar under which the hunter was resting. He came forward slowly, as if knowing by instinct that all was not right.

At first Peaceful Jones was alarmed, then a sudden grim smile came to his bronzed features. He drew his long hunting knife and waited for the bear to come within striking distance.

"Your life or mine—an' it ain't goin' to be me ef I kin help it," he muttered to himself.

The bear came to the cedar and pushed a branch aside with his nose. Like lightning, Peaceful Jones leaped forward and made a plunge with his hunting knife. Then the blade was withdrawn and slashed rapidly across the animal's throat. There was a grunt, a gasp, and the animal fell down in its tracks, gave a convulsive shudder, and lay dead.

Weak as he was, the old trapper managed to draw the game under the cedar and kicked some fresh snow over the spot where the blood had flowed. Then he took his hunting knife, cut out a piece of bear meat, and began to suck and gnaw upon it like some wild animal. It was a primitive meal, and might have made another person sick, but it satisfied him and gave him strength,— and strength was what he needed above anything else.

The morning brought a light snowstorm, for which he was thankful, since it would cover up his tracks. As soon as he felt able to do so, he cut himself a big chunk of the bear meat, slung it over his shoulder, and set off, in the direction of the Kinotah. He plunged directly into the great forest, afraid to take to any of the trails leading eastward for fear he would run into the enemy once again.

CHAPTER XIX
THE SHOOTING CONTEST

To Dave and Henry, left at Fort Pitt, the days passed slowly. Occasionally they went out hunting, with fair success, but, warned by Captain Ecuyer, did not venture far away. They waited patiently for some word from Rodney, and some word from Dave's father, but no news came to them.

"I hope Rodney got home in safety," said Henry, one day. "I don't see why we don't hear from him."

"I wish father would send some word," answered Dave. "I am beginning to grow anxious."

October slipped into November, and winter was now on them in earnest. It snowed a great deal, and Fort Pitt was cut off from communication in all directions. The soldiers scarcely knew what to do with themselves, and the settlers who had gone to the stronghold for protection were also weary of the confinement.

To pass the time some of the men one day got up a shooting contest, and asked Dave and Henry to join. The youths were willing, and paid the admission fee, two shillings. The first prize was a silver mug, the second prize a fancy bullet-mold, and the third a new hunting knife.

Among the soldiers to participate in the contest were two named Gasway and Pelton. Both were beefy Englishmen, from London, who had come over the year before. Each was given to boasting, and each felt certain of winning either the first or the second prize.

"What! you boys going to compete!" cried Gasway, to Dave, disdainfully. "Sure, 'twill be good money thrown away."

"Perhaps we'll not do so badly," said Dave, nettled by Gasway's superior manner.

"The first prize will go to me and the second to my friend Pelton," went on the English soldier. "I take it you chits will be at the end of the list."

Left to himself, Dave sought out his cousin and told him what Gasway had said. Henry smiled grimly.

"He had better do his crowing after the shooting, not before, Dave."

"I wish we could beat him, and beat Pelton, too."

"Well, we can try."

The contest was to come off on the following afternoon. The day proved clear, and a goodly number of those stationed at the fort gathered to witness the shooting. The target, a large affair of wood, with several rings and a bull's-eye, was nailed to a tree, and a stump marked the spot where each contestant must stand while shooting. Each contestant was to have three shots, and the highest possible score was eighteen points.

The first soldier to shoot, a man named Pepperley, made two points with his first shot. Another made three, and another five. Then came Gasway, who made five also, and Pelton, who made six.

"Now, Dave," said Henry, and Dave stepped to the front, took careful aim, and pulled the trigger.

"Four!" announced the officer who was keeping the tally.

Dave was a trifle disappointed, as he had hoped to make at least five. Yet he managed to smile as he turned to Henry.

"You can do better than that, I know," he said.

Two other marksmen now came to the front, making four each. Then it was Henry's turn.

The youth took his time about shooting, and when the smoke cleared away a shout went up:

"A bull's-eye for Henry Morris!"

"Good—that counts six for you, Henry!" exclaimed Dave.

"A bull's-eye for Henry Morris!"

Soon the men were shooting for the second time. Dave got a bull's-eye and Henry a five, giving them 10 and 11 respectively. Strange to say Gasway and Pelton also scored 10 and 11, so the friends on each side were a tie. The other marksmen got from 8 to 10 each.

Those to make the highest scores were to shoot last, and as a consequence Dave was pitted against a soldier named Brocaw and against Gasway, while Henry was pitted against Pelton.

Brocaw was the first to shoot and made a four, much to his disgust.

"You go next," said Gasway to Dave.

"Toss up for it," said the officer who was judging the contest, and the toss of a penny sent Gasway to the front. He was a trifle nervous and took so long to shoot that some friends jeered at him.

"Five!" called out the judge, when the shot had been taken.

"Now, Dave, make a bull's-eye!" cried Henry.

It must be confessed that Dave was also nervous, although he did his best to conceal it. This time he raised his rifle quickly and blazed away before anybody expected it.

"A bull's-eye, sure enough!"

"That gives him two points above Brocaw and one point above Gasway!"

The toss of the penny now brought Pelton to the front, and he shot with great care, yet all he could make was a five, which gave him a total of 16 points, just what Dave had.

"Now, Henry, a bull's-eye sure," said Dave.

"More likely he'll make a three," sneered Gasway. He was disgusted because of his own showing.

Henry was cool, for his nerves seldom bothered him. He took aim with great deliberation, and hit the target exactly in the center.

"Seventeen points for Henry Morris!" was the cry.

"He takes the first prize!"

"He certainly can shoot, even if he is young."

It was decided that Dave Morris and Ike Pelton should have one more shot each, the one coming nearest to the center of the target taking the second prize and the other taking the third prize. The toss made Pelton shoot first. All of the other shots on the target were chalked over, so that there might be no mistakes in scoring.

This time Pelton took more care than ever in shooting, and as a consequence put his bullet directly on the inner ring,—something which, though between 5 and 6, would count the higher number.

"I fancy the youngster can't beat that," said Gasway.

"Don't be so sure," answered a soldier who favored Dave.

Dave's heart thumped loudly in his breast as he stepped up beside the tree-stump. But he kept outwardly calm and did what he could to steady his arms. He took one good look at the target, raised his rifle, and fired. The smoke cleared away and there was a second of silence.

"A miss!"

"What!" cried Dave and Henry, in a breath.

"The bullet does not seem to have touched the target," announced the judge.

"Oh, I must have hit the target!" went on Dave. "Why, I aimed as carefully as before, when I made 16 in three shots."

"Can't help it. The target has not been touched. You can see for yourself."

Dave ran forward, and so did all of the others. There was Pelton's shot and all of the others', each marked with chalk.

"I know wot he did!" shouted one old frontiersman.

"And so do I!" added Henry, triumphantly. "It's been done before, too."

"What?" came in a chorus.

"His bullet is on top of mine, directly in the center of the bull's-eye."

"Can that be possible?" cried the officer in charge. "We'll soon see."

He got out his penknife and began to dig at the hole in the middle of the target. Soon one bullet came up, and another was revealed beneath it.

"Dave Morris gets the second prize, and Pelton takes third!"

"And Gasway and the others get nothing," said one of the soldiers. "Gasway, maybe you won't blow so much after this."

"Bah! The shooting didn't amount to much anyway!" growled Gasway, and lost no time in getting out of sight. But he never said anything more to Dave or Henry about target shooting, nor did Pelton mention the subject.

After that Henry was urged to try his hand at long-distance shooting. To please his friends he complied, and made several remarkable shots, which called forth praise from Captain Ecuyer and many others.

"I know of nobody who can shoot better than you," said the commandant of the fort.

"I know one man who can—the man who taught me," answered the youth.

"And who is he?"

"Sam Barringford. I don't know if he can do any better at a target, but he can best me in shooting at running game or flying birds. He is remarkably quick that way."

"But you must be able to hit a bird on the wing."

"I can generally. Once in a while I miss," answered Henry.

"But not often," said Dave. "He is the best hunter in our family, by a good deal," he added, warmly.

"Well, you can do a little too," said Captain Ecuyer, with a laugh.

The shooting had taken place in a clearing behind Fort Pitt. The party was about to return to the fort, when a sudden shouting was heard.

"What is the matter?" asked Captain Ecuyer, quickly.

"Somebody is coming down the trail!"

"A messenger! A messenger!" was the cry.

"It is Peaceful Jones!"

The report proved true; it was indeed Peaceful Jones who was coming along the trail leading from the west. He walked slowly, as if very tired or full of pain.

"Let's go to meet him!" cried Dave, and ran forward, followed by Henry and half a dozen others. It did not take them long to reach the trapper, who, as soon as he saw them, stopped short and clutched a tree for support.

"What is it, Jones?" asked Henry, and then started, as did Dave, for they saw the man was very thin, as if he had suffered from a long illness.

"Thank Heaven I—I am ba—back at last!" gasped Peaceful Jones. "I th— thought I'd never ma—make it!"

"You are sick—you have been hurt!" burst out Dave, and helped to support him.

"Yes—got shot—Bevoir's crowd—got away—sick—lost in forest— Indians—old medicine man—got away again—come here—and now——" Peaceful Jones could not go on.

"You were shot?" queried Dave; "and by Bevoir's crowd? What of my father?" And the youth's heart seemed to stop beating.

"Dead—everybody is dead but me, and I—I—oh!" And then Peaceful Jones dropped limply into the arms of Dave and Henry. His eyes closed, and for the time being he knew no more.

"He has fainted from exhaustion," said an under officer who had come up. "Carry him to the fort, and we will do what we can to revive him. He must have important news to tell."

"Yes," said Dave, brokenly. The mist was swimming before his eyes. "Oh, Henry, can this be true? Can father be dead?"

"Let us hope for the best," answered his cousin. He, too, could hardly speak.

Then some soldiers raised Peaceful Jones to their shoulders and marched off to the fort with him. Dave and Henry followed in their rear, each with a heart that sank lower and lower at every step.

CHAPTER XX
ANOTHER LONG JOURNEY

For several hours Peaceful Jones lay in a stupor of pain and exhaustion. He was given the best medical attention the fort afforded, and at last dropped into a deep sleep, from which he did not awaken until the next day. He was then still weak, but able to tell his story in detail.

Much of it we already know. After leaving the vicinity of the cedar with his bear meat over his shoulder he had wandered around in the woods and gotten lost. Then he had been snowed in for over a week, and at the end of that period had been taken down with a fever, and had come out of it to find himself in an Indian camp and under the care of a medicine man for whom he had once done a favor. The medicine man told him that some other Indians wished to kill him, and at the first opportunity the trapper had fled from the Indian village and started again for Fort Pitt. He had fallen over some rocks into a hollow while on the last three miles of his journey and was so weak that he could hardly stand when discovered by his friends.

"But are you certain the others were all killed—that my father was killed?" asked Dave.

"He must be dead, Dave—although I didn't see him go down. I was outside of the tradin' post. But I heard a Frenchman and an Indian speak about it. They were more than anxious to kill me too."

"Oh, I cannot believe that father is dead!" burst out the youth, and had to turn away to hide his tears.

Henry did what he could to comfort his cousin, but was himself much downcast. That evening the pair talked the matter over for several hours, but the discussion did not appear to help the situation.

"I wish we could get Colonel Bouquet or Captain Ecuyer to march against Jean Bevoir," said Dave. "That Frenchman and his associates ought to be shot down or hanged."

"I don't think either the colonel or the captain will want to go out during the winter," answered Henry, which was a correct conclusion. The season was proving so severe that the idea of sending a body of soldiers on a trail that was then but little known was out of the question, in the opinion of both the colonel and the commandant of the fort. Both said nothing could be done until spring.

"I don't believe they will ever send the soldiers out there," said Dave to Henry, with much bitterness in his tone. "They think they have their hands full taking care of matters as far west as this fort."

"Well, we can't exactly blame them, Dave. They have had some hard times here, during the past few years."

"But do you want to stay here and let Bevoir and his crowd escape punishment?"

"I certainly do not. But what can we do? It would be foolhardy for us to dream of going out there alone."

"We might go home and organize a party from there. I think your father would help us."

"That is a roundabout way of getting at it," answered Henry, thoughtfully. "But it could be done."

"I can't bear to think of staying here and doing nothing," resumed Dave. "Why, every day would seem like a month! I must know the truth, and I must do something to bring Jean Bevoir and those other rascals to justice."

With Dave, to think was to act, and by the next day he had made up his mind fully. He would return to Will's Creek, tell his Uncle Joe and the others all, and get them to aid him in organizing an expedition to move against Jean Bevoir and his evil associates.

The commandant of the fort was much surprised at the youth's determination and secretly admired his pluck. Yet he shrugged his shoulders over the wisdom of the plan.

"'Tis a long journey to the east and 'twill be a longer journey to the west," he said. "However, have your own way, and I will aid you as much as I can."

It was arranged that two frontiersmen named Lawson and Devine should accompany Dave and Henry on their journey eastward. The four were to go on foot, taking along snowshoes, and each was to carry a knapsack well filled with rations. They were to move along as quickly as possible, only stopping to shoot game when it was absolutely necessary.

Lawson and Devine were fairly well known to the youths. Each had been over the trail a number of times, and each was stout and strong and well able to resist the hardships of the trip. All went over their outfits with care, and did not carry anything more than seemed absolutely necessary.

The start was made from Fort Pitt on a bright clear day in the middle of December. A few of the soldiers went out to see them off, and to the first bend in the trail. Then they turned back, and the party of four was left to confront whatever lay before it.

"I do not think we shall meet any Indians," said Henry. "They do not fancy moving around in such nipping weather as this."

"Keep your eyes open, is what I say," answered Lawson, who was striding along in advance. "An Injun ain't going to announce his coming with bells and a horn."

For the first few miles of the journey but little was spoken, the frontiersmen being of a silent turn of mind and Dave and Henry being busy with their thoughts. They were following the old Braddock road, thinking they might make better progress on this through the heavy snows than on the General Forbes route.

"I am afraid, if we push ourselves too much the first day, we'll be rather stiff the second," remarked Henry, as they stopped for a minute on a rise of ground to get their breath.

"Oh, I want to make as many miles as I possibly can," answered Dave impatiently.

"I agree with Henry," said Devine. "We'll have to take it a bit easier. We'll gain by it in the end, mark my words."

That night they encamped in a snug spot among the rocks. Plenty of firewood was handy, and they built up a roaring blaze. On the way Henry had seen a bunch of rabbits and had not resisted the temptation to take a shot. He had secured three, and these were cooked to a turn and eaten, after which they turned in without delay, each taking his turn at standing guard and keeping up the fire.

The next day was largely a repetition of the first, and the third day was on the same order, although Lawson saw a deer and shot at it, breaking its leg. Dave gave the game a finishing bullet, and they took the meat to their next camping spot. There the deer was cut up, and each was given a good-sized piece to carry along.

"That ought to last us several days," said Lawson. "So we won't have to waste time or powder on more stuff for the larder."

The next day, about noon, came an alarm. Turning a bend of the trail they came in sight of fully a score of Indians, all on snowshoes and journeying in the direction of Fort Pitt.

"Out of sight!" warned Lawson, and leaped behind some bushes, followed by his companions.

"I think they saw us first," said Henry. "And if so, it will do us small good to hide."

He had hardly spoken when a shrill whistle filled the air, followed by a cry that was well known to Dave and Henry. At once both boys ran out into the road.

"White Buffalo!" cried Dave, and moved onward to greet the aged chief.

"Where goes my young friend?" questioned White Buffalo.

"I am going home," answered Dave, and then told of what had happened at the trading post. White Buffalo was much concerned.

"'Tis sad news indeed," said he. "And comes at a time when White Buffalo's heart was filled with gladness."

"What has happened to make you glad?" asked Henry.

"My tribe is at peace once more. Henceforth all of our warriors will be friendly to the English. And they have made me the chief of all my people."

"I am glad of that, for your sake!" cried Dave. "And you deserve this, White Buffalo, for you are the very best Indian I know."

"White Buffalo wishes he could aid his friend Dave," said the Indian. "But now he must journey to the home of the Delawares, to prepare for the great ceremonial. But when he is at liberty he will follow Dave, and bring with him some of his best braves."

"I'll be glad of that, White Buffalo."

"If Bevoir and his curs have slain Dave's father and his friends they must suffer for it," went on the aged chief. "And the trading post belongs to Dave and his people," he added, firmly. "Neither the French nor the red men can have it."

A talk lasting an hour followed, and White Buffalo said again that sooner or later he would aid Dave. How he kept his word we shall see in a later chapter.

The Indians went on their way, and once again Dave and the others turned their faces eastward. Nothing more happened to alarm them, and thus they went on for two days more.

"We'll soon be there," said Dave. "We ought to strike one of the settlements in a day or two." They had certainly pushed ahead with rapidity, as their strained and tired legs testified.

That night they encamped among some trees, and in the morning found everything covered with snow. The snow was still coming down steadily.

"We are not going to do so well to-day," said Henry. "We must take care, or we'll get off the trail."

"Trust me to keep to the trail," said Lawson. "I know the ground too well to get lost."

It was indeed hard to go on, and by noon they were glad enough to stop for a long rest. The wind was biting cold and the temperature was going down rapidly.

"Unless I miss my guess we're going to have an awful night," remarked Devine. "The best thing we can do is to find some good shelter before it gets too dark."

They pushed on from two o'clock to four. By that time the leaden sky was growing dark, and they looked around for the best shelter obtainable. At last they chose a spot where there were some rocks and thickly set trees.

"This isn't as good as it might be, but it's the best around here, I reckon," said Lawson.

They scraped away the snow and built a fire, and then heaped up some brushwood as a shelter from the wind. But it kept growing colder and colder, until they were glad enough to huddle close to the blaze with their coats buttoned closely around them.

"This is going to be a banner night," said Henry, and his words proved correct, so far as the cold was concerned. The temperature dropped steadily until two o'clock in the morning, when Dave felt as if he was "breathing icicles" as he expressed it. It was so cold that nobody could sleep, and they spent the time in hugging the fire and in drinking hot coffee. The two men had a bottle of liquor, of which they consumed not a little. The liquor was offered to the two youths, but each declined.

"I think we are better off without it," said Dave, and Henry said the same.

CHAPTER XXI
A NEW MOVE

All were glad to see the sun rise in the morning. The storm had cleared away, the wind had fallen, and gradually the temperature rose once more.

"That was a night to remember," said Henry. "I don't want to be out in anything colder."

"Nor I," answered his cousin. "Had it not been for the roaring fire and the hot coffee we might have been frozen to death."

"I'd rather have my liquor than the coffee," said Devine.

"I don't agree with you," said Dave. "Liquor may heat you up for awhile, but it will make you colder afterwards."

They were glad enough to break camp and walk just for the sake of getting warm. But they were all more or less sleepy, and in the middle of the day each dozed off after dinner. That night they found a well-sheltered spot, and got a rest that did them a world of good. The weather was still cold, but not as freezing as it had been.

It was not until two days later that they reached the first of the settlements, and after that they slept each night in either a log cabin or some other shelter. The folks they met were glad to do what they could for them, although this was but little, as the Indian war had left them all comparatively poor.

"I've got to start just where I began twelve years ago," said one old settler. "The Injuns didn't leave me a thing but this old cow-shed. We've got to build a new cabin, and buy some stock, and do a mountain o' work to get the place into shape again." And his position was that of hundreds of others. Many had left the frontier entirely, not caring to make a living where there was so much danger.

Another slight snowstorm was encountered, but the party kept on steadily, and soon came within sight of Will's Creek. Then, one clear afternoon, both Dave and Henry set up a loud shout:

"Rodney!"

"Hello!" was the answer, and Rodney, who was out hunting, turned to them in great amazement. "Dave and Henry! How in the world did you get here?"

"Walked," answered Henry. "How are all the folks at home?"

"Everybody is doing very well. But this is certainly a surprise. Come along to the house. The folks will be wild to see you, mother especially," and Rodney gave Henry a meaning glance.

They soon reached the log cabin, and all at the place rushed out to give them a warm greeting. Mrs. Morris kissed her son several times and then kissed Dave, and little Nell also came in for her share of caresses.

"I certainly did not expect you at this season," said Joseph Morris. "Perhaps you have brought some sort of a message?" and he looked inquiringly at his son and his nephew.

"It's about father," said Dave. He tried to go on, but his voice choked up and he motioned for Henry to speak.

Henry told the tale of the disaster at the trading post, just as it had been related by Peaceful Jones. Mr. Morris and the others listened with keen interest. Mrs. Morris burst into tears and Nell did likewise.

"Dave, I am so sorry for you!" cried his aunt, as she hugged the youth to her breast.

"And so am I!" burst out Nell. "Oh, that wicked, wicked Jean Bevoir!"

"I do not wonder that you wished to bring the news home," said Joseph Morris. "It is a fearful state of affairs. The fight must have been a losing one from the start. Peaceful Jones can be thankful that he escaped."

"I wanted to go to the trading post—to get somebody from the fort to go," said Dave, brokenly. "But no one in command would take the responsibility."

"It is because of the rumors that are afloat," answered his uncle. "Some say Pontiac is going to do his best to capture Fort Pitt and every place west of Fort Detroit."

The whole evening was spent in discussing the situation, Dave and Henry going over matters just as they had at the fort. It was a sober home-coming, and none of the older folks thought of going to bed until late. Lawson and Devine were told to make themselves at home.

"Sam Barringford has gone to Fort Cumberland on business," said Joseph Morris, in reply to an inquiry from Henry. "He will be back to-morrow or the day after."

The next day matters were talked over once more, and Dave told his uncle that nothing would satisfy him but to make the effort to reach the trading post and learn the truth concerning his parent.

"Well, I do not blame you, Dave," answered his uncle. "But to get out there from here will be no easy matter, and to go alone or with only a handful of men would be folly. By this time Jean Bevoir has probably put the post in a good state of defense, and, since Jones escaped, he must be on constant guard."

"I have a little plan to suggest, Uncle Joe. Why cannot we travel almost to the post and then go into quarters somewhere and send one or two men out in quiet? The men might go to the post, pretend to be friendly with Bevoir, and state that Peaceful Jones is dead, having been found so in the woods. Bevoir may then expose his plans and relax his vigilance, and we can watch our chances, rush in, and take possession."

This plan appealed strongly to Henry, and even Mr. Morris nodded as if he approved. Still, there were many things to consider, the planter told his nephew, and he wanted a few days to deliberate. That night he talked it over in private with his wife.

"Dave wants to find out the truth about his father, Lucy," said the planter. "I do not blame him, and I want to find out the truth myself, and see that justice is done. If he goes out to the trading post I feel it will be my duty to go with him."

"But, Joseph, I do not wish to stay here alone!" cried Mrs. Morris. "Remember, I have not only Nell but the twins to take care of!"

"Henry will want to go with Dave, since they are like brothers," continued Joseph Morris. "But Rodney can remain here, and so can some of the neighbors, if you wish it."

"And would you go out there alone with the boys?"

"No! no! by no means! I should want to organize a regular expedition, and have the men sworn into regular army service at the fort. Then, when the time came, we could deal with Bevoir and his men in true military style."

"You must have been doing a deal of thinking about this, Joseph?"

"And why not? James was my only living brother, and he was very dear to me."

"And he was dear to me too, and I think of Dave as of a son. But I hate to see you leave, just when we thought we might settle down again as of old."

"Poor Dave will never have any peace of mind until he knows the exact truth."

"True! My heart aches for him. Well, Joseph, do as you think best. But, for my sake, do not be rash!" And then Mrs. Morris kissed her husband affectionately.

The next day Sam Barringford came back from Fort Cumberland. He too was surprised to see the new arrivals and greatly shocked over the news they had brought.

"The skunk! The dirty skunk!" cried the frontiersman, referring to Jean Bevoir. "Oh, just wait till I git my paws on him, thet's all!" And his big frame shook with emotion. He was willing to start for the post at any time and under any conditions.

Barringford had brought in news that interested the Morrises as much, almost, as it did himself. At Fort Cumberland he had met a French-Englishman, who had just arrived from Detroit. This gentleman knew something about Maurice Hamilton, the father of the twins, and said that Mr. Hamilton was not in England but in this country, although exactly where he could not tell. He had started for London by way of New York, but had then changed his mind and gone to Philadelphia.

"As soon as I heard thet, I sent a letter to Philadelphia," said Sam Barringford. "If he's thar he'll most likely git it and write back, or come on."

"I hope he does come on," said Mrs. Morris. "I should like to see what the father of Tom and Artie looks like."

"I don't want Tom and Artie to go away," pouted Nell. "I love them and I want them to stay here."

"Well, they are not going away just yet," said Rodney, to quiet his sister.

During the winter a great many trappers and frontiersmen remained close to the forts and settlements, so it was comparatively easy for Joseph Morris and Dave to organize the expedition that was to start for the trading post on the Ohio. The company was organized upon military lines, with Joseph Morris as captain, and Dave and Henry as first and second lieutenants. It was composed of eighteen men, all well versed in shooting and in scouting. As an old army sharpshooter, Sam Barringford was placed in charge of the advance guard. The company took along a pack-train of twelve horses, each animal carrying only such articles as were deemed necessary for the trip. The men were told why the expedition had been formed, and each promised to stand by Mr. Morris to the end.

While the preparations were being made, the holidays came and went, but only Nell and the twins received any gifts, the minds of the older folks being filled with other matters.

"I couldn't celebrate Christmas if I tried," said Dave to Henry. "In fact, I couldn't celebrate anything. All I want to do is to find out the truth about father."

"And bring Jean Bevoir, Benoit Vascal, and those rascally Indians to justice," added Henry, who always looked at the practical side of affairs.

It had been arranged that Asa Dobson and his wife should remain at the Morris homestead for the time being, and also an old colored man known as Pompey Sugg. Pompey was a fine shot, and said he would keep a constant guard against Indians.

"Dar ain't no Injuns gwine ter git de best ob dis chicken," said the colored man. "If da come nosin' around hyer Pomp will gib 'em a dose ob buckshot, ki hi!" And he laughed as if shooting Indians was the best joke in the world. He was known to be a faithful fellow, and Joseph Morris placed great reliance on him.

The expedition was gotten together at Fort Cumberland, but the actual start was from the Morris homestead. Here, many men and women gathered to see the party off, and numerous were the handshakes and well-wishes. Dave received a warm embrace from his aunt.

"Keep up your courage," she whispered into his ear. "Remember, Dave, I shall always be a mother to you, and your Uncle Joseph will be a father."

"Yes, I know, Aunt Lucy, and you are very kind," he answered. He would have said more, but the words stuck in his throat.

"Take good care o' the twins!" called out Sam Barringford. And then he gave each a tight hug, for he did not know but that their father would be along to take them away before his return.

"Good-bye, Lucy," said Joseph Morris, to his wife, as he gave her a last embrace. "Remember, I shall be back again as soon as possible. Do not worry while I am away."

"How can I help but worry?" she answered, through her tears. "The West is such a wild country, and the Indians and those wicked Frenchmen are so cruel! If you give them the chance, they will kill you, and all of the others, too, just as they did brother James and his party!"

"We shall try to be careful."

Everything was now in readiness for the start, and at the command from Joseph Morris the men fell into place and set off, the pack-horses with their drivers occupying the middle of the little train. The boundless West and the mighty forest lay before them. Would they succeed or fail in their mission?

CHAPTER XXII
A FIGHT AMONG WILD BEASTS

"There is no use in talking, this is certainly slow traveling. If it wasn't for the pack-horses we could get along twice as fast."

It was Henry who spoke, and he addressed his father. The pair were trudging along the snow-clad trail, with Dave and Sam Barringford slightly in advance. It was a mild, clear day in January, with the sun kissing every mound of white and causing it to glitter as if with diamonds.

The little expedition had been on the march four days, and all evidence of civilization had been left behind. They were taking what Sam Barringford and two of the other frontiersmen considered a "short cut" on the route to Fort Pitt. Whether or not they would stop at the fort when they arrived in that vicinity was still an open question. On the one hand, they did not wish to lose the time to do so, and on the other, they wanted to make certain that no news from the West had come to the stronghold during their absence.

So far they had seen no trace of the Indians—indeed, they had met no strangers of any kind. The loneliness of the wilderness winter was on all sides of them. Sometimes they journeyed for hours through the untracked snow without a single sound disturbing them. At times this oppressiveness was hard on Dave and caused him to grow so "blue" that he hardly knew what to do. Henry tried to cheer him up, but with little success.

The frontiersmen were all of the silent kind—their calling had rendered them so—and conversation dragged, enlivened only now and then by the talk of the men who urged along the horses. The steeds did their best, but the footing was uncertain, and more than once they went down into pitfalls partly covered with snow and had to be hauled out by main strength.

"The Injuns have certainly left this neighborhood," observed Sam Barringford, after another spell of silence. "Not a sign on 'em anywhere."

"I am glad of that," answered Joseph Morris. "I want to meet nobody until we arrive at Fort Pitt or the trading post."

"When I war to Fort Cumberland I heard a report about Pontiac," went on the old frontiersman. "They said he war goin' west—to stir up the redskins along the Mississippi and lower Ohio, to make another attack on the English. It war said the French trappers an' traders would help him."

"Such a thing is possible," answered Joseph Morris. "Of one thing I am certain: Pontiac will not rest until he has either won a victory or been killed."

It was true that Pontiac was again active, this time close to the banks of the Illinois River. Here he essayed to unite the western tribes against the English,—a work that availed him little.

The Indian uprisings at Fort Pitt, Detroit, and other points had created a terrible feeling against the red men in all portions of the Colonies, but this hatred was most bitter in Pennsylvania, especially in Paxton township, where a large body of settlers of Irish and Scotch blood organized themselves into a command popularly known as the Paxton Boys. This command hunted down the Indians on all sides, and even slaughtered a harmless tribe, living under the protection of some Moravian missionaries.

"Down with all redskins!" was their cry, and they moved upon Lancaster, where some Indians had taken refuge in the workhouse. The doors were battered down and all of the Indians slain, and then the Paxton Boys marched down to Philadelphia, to capture some of the enemy who had fled to that city. To hold the maddened frontiersmen in check, Benjamin Franklin aided in forming a body of militia, and these compelled the Paxton Boys to leave without further bloodshed. The killing of the friendly Indians was looked upon by the law-abiding citizens as an outrage and the feeling against the Paxton Boys was very bitter. On their side, the Paxton Boys contended that the Indians had all proved treacherous more or less and that "the only good Indian was the dead Indian,"—a saying that soon became a household word among a certain class of the communities.

In many cases, after the meeting at Johnson Hall, the Indians were compelled to give up their captives, and this brought on numerous affecting scenes. Some women and children had been separated from their people for several years, and had made warm ties among the Indians. A number had even married red men and had children, and these did not want to separate from their husbands. Some little children had completely forgotten their real parents, and when taken from the Indians cried loudly, much to the distress of their mothers and fathers.

"Look! look!" cried one poor woman. "My own child, my Bessie, does not know me!"

"And look you!" said one man. "My Johanna has married an Indian and they have two children! I would rather she were dead!" And the settler turned and would have nothing more to do with his own flesh and blood. Tradition says of this man that in years after the Indian husband of his daughter saved him from being massacred during an uprising, and he was taken to safety by a grandson whom he had disowned.

One day after another went by, and still the expedition under Joseph Morris wended its way westward through the wilderness. So far the weather had remained fine, but at the end of a week it began to thaw and then there set in a misty rain, disagreeable in the extreme. The trail was sloppy, and if a person slipped down he was bound to get wet through and through.

"This is fine weather in which to catch cold," grumbled Henry. The only thing he objected to when being out was rain.

During the rain and mist, which lasted for two whole days, they made but slow progress. Each night they went into camp early, and spent several hours in getting dry and making themselves half comfortable.

On the morning of the day when it cleared off, Henry and Dave were in advance, in company with Sam Barringford. They were looking for game, and hoped to stir up some rabbits, if not something larger.

"I see some partridges!" cried Henry, presently, and was about to take aim, when a sudden loud snapping and snarling broke upon the air, coming from the forest on their left.

"Wild animals!" cried Dave. "Don't you think so, Sam?"

"I do," was the short answer. "Come on an' see wot they be."

The old frontiersman led the way, and soon the party of three came upon a scene that thrilled them with interest.

In a little glade in the forest lay a dead deer, the blood still pouring from a big bite in the throat. Close at hand were a small panther and a full-grown wildcat, tightly locked together, and biting and snapping in the most vicious manner possible. At one moment the wildcat would be on top, then the panther, and then they would roll over and over, the snow and fur flying in all directions. The blood was flowing from a gash in the panther's side and the wildcat's left ear was slitted into shreds.

"Here is a fight surely!" whispered Barringford. "They mean business, they do!"

"What shall we do?" whispered Dave. The sight thrilled him to the core.

"Let 'em have it out, lad—ain't no ust to interfere in sech a muss as thet."

The two animals were certainly "having it out." Over and over they went and the fur continued to fly. The wildcat now had the panther by the neck, while the latter was twisted half around and was clawing frantically, trying to reach its enemy's vitals.

"Looks as if the wildcat would get the best of it," observed Henry. But at that moment the larger beast shook the hold of the other, and swinging around caught the wildcat in the stomach with its claws. Then the wildcat closed in with another snarl, catching the panther in the lower jaw. It was a death-like grip that could not be shaken, and the animals fell over on their sides. The fur and snow continued to fly, but both animals soon grew weaker. There was a last struggle, a gasp from the wildcat, and then that animal stretched out dead. The hold on the panther's jaw relaxed and slowly the panther staggered up. It went but a few steps, then fell down, gave a grunt or two, and began to kick feebly.

"Both on 'em done fer!" said Sam Barringford. "It war certainly a great fight."

"The painter ain't dead yet!" cried Henry. "Look out!"

They turned and saw that the panther was trying to get up. It had discovered the intruders and wanted to fight. It gave a feeble leap, but failed to reach them.

"I'll fix thet painter," murmured Barringford, and drew his hunting knife.

"Don't touch him—let him go," pleaded Dave. "He made such a good fight against the wildcat." The panther had turned towards the bushes. Now it slunk out of sight, so weak that it could scarcely drag one foot after another. Before they left the spot they saw the animal breathe its last.

They examined the deer and found it had suffered nothing but the gaping wound in the throat, made evidently by the wildcat.

"This is a prize," said Henry. "It saves us the trouble of shooting one."

"I suppose the wildcat brought the deer down and the painter wanted to steal it," said Dave. "It's a pretty good-sized deer for a wildcat to tackle."

"I reckon as how the wildcat war half starved an' got desprit," spoke up the old frontiersman. "He must have jumped down on the deer from some tree and hung on till the deer war dead."

The others had by this time come up, and they looked at the deer with interest. The game was slung over the back of one of the horses and the onward march resumed. That night all enjoyed the fresh venison.

On the following day they came to a fair-sized river, and there encamped for their noonday repast. Taking an axe, Henry cut a round hole in the ice and brought forth his fishing lines.

"Going to try fishing, eh?" said Dave. "All right, I'll do what I can to help."

They soon had their lines ready, and baiting up, allowed them to sink through the hole. The fish were sluggish, and for a long time they got no bite. But then came a lazy tug, and hauling in, Henry brought up a fat fish that weighed all of two pounds.

"Good for you, Henry!" cried his cousin. "You always were lucky at this sort of thing."

"Not always," answered Henry, grimly. "I have fished through the ice more than once and caught next to nothing."

"I'll never forget how I once brought up a snake and then fell into the water," went on Dave, recalling an incident already related in detail in this series. "No more snakes for me. I hate——Gracious! Look at that! A snake as sure as you're born!"

Dave's line and hook came up. On the end was something dark and slimy. Henry started back and then gave a laugh.

"Only an old tree-root, Dave!" he cried, merrily. "Don't holler before you are hurt."

"I was thinking of that other snake," answered his cousin, somewhat sheepishly. He dropped in his hook again. "Hope I get a bite this time."

His wish was gratified. Fishing proved so good that the youths persuaded Mr. Morris to let them continue for awhile, and in less than an hour they had a full mess for supper. The men enjoyed the change greatly, and told Henry and Dave they could go fishing at every river the expedition crossed.

CHAPTER XXIII
THE RESCUE OF THE STRANGER

A few days later brought the expedition to Fort Pitt. Captain Ecuyer was surprised to see Dave and Henry back so soon, and praised them for the rapid time they had made. But he shook his head when he listened to the further plans of the party.

"I believe you are taking a great risk," said he. "I have been sending out scouts within the last week, and their reports are far from satisfactory. They have seen Indians at a distance, and there is not the slightest doubt but that this stronghold is being watched closely."

"It is queer then that we were not attacked in coming here," answered Joseph Morris. "We kept a careful watch, but saw no enemy."

"Perhaps your guard saved you," said the commandant of the fort. "But, remember, it will be different when you go westward from here. The Indians are surely gathering in the West, and what they intend to do, Heaven alone knows. Were I you I should at least wait until spring before venturing further."

Dave would not listen to this, and Henry sided with his impatient cousin, knowing well how anxious Dave was to learn the truth concerning his father. Joseph Morris realized the situation, and it must be admitted that he, too, was anxious, since his brother had been very dear to him. A consultation was held, and it was resolved that the expedition should rest at Fort Pitt until over Sunday—four days—and then push forward as before.

The coming of the expedition to Fort Pitt brought a smile to the face of Peaceful Jones, who was slowly recovering from the privation to which he had been exposed.

"It's an outright shame I can't go with ye!" said the old trapper, with a profound sigh. "Wouldn't like no better fun nor to lick Jean Bevoir an' his crowd good!"

"Don't worry about thet, Peaceful," answered Sam Barringford. "Only give us the chance an' we'll lick Bevoir an' his crowd good an' proper, believe me!"

"Thet feller ain't fit to be on this airth, Sam—he's wuss nor a snake in the grass!"

"I agree with ye, Peaceful, an' when I git through with him he'll be wuss off nor any snake ye ever heard tell on," concluded the old frontiersman.

From Fort Pitt the expedition took to the trail James Morris had followed in journeying to his trading post. The January thaw was a thing of the past, and once again cold weather, with several heavy falls of snow, reigned supreme. The trail was in spots all but impassable, and on more than one occasion they had to literally dig the horses out of the drifts into which they wandered. Twice they had to go into camp for two days at a time—to rest up and wait for the skies to clear. It was a wearisome and courage-testing journey, as even stout-limbed Sam Barringford testified.

"It's pure grit an' nuthin else is goin' to carry us through," said he. "Fer this travelin' ain't fit fer a dog."

"There is one comfort,—it is keeping the Indians away from us," answered Joseph Morris. "They won't venture very far from their villages in this sort of weather."

But Joseph Morris was mistaken. All unknown to the whites, the red men were watching their movements closely. Even though the expedition had left Fort Pitt under cover of darkness the Indians had discovered them on the western trail early in the morning, and now speedy runners were carrying the news to various villages for fifty miles around.

Soon a counter expedition, under Eagle Nose,—a well-known Maumee River warrior,—was sent out, to do battle with the coming white men. The Indians in this detachment numbered about thirty warriors, all young and eager to fight. They advanced over the snow on snowshoes, and as soon as they came up to the trail of Joseph Morris's expedition went into hiding.

"Let us wait until the hated English sleep," said Eagle Nose. "Then we can kill them all and take their goods and horses back to our lodges with us." It may be mentioned here that it was Eagle Nose and his men who had, the year before, fallen on an English detachment near Venango and murdered all the soldiers, mutilating some of the bodies most horribly. For this Eagle Nose became afterwards known as the Red Butcher,—an appellation that clung to him to the day of his death.

On the afternoon that the Indians came upon the trail of the whites, Sam Barringford set out on a hunt, taking Dave and Henry with him. A halt had been made, to rest up before climbing through a hollow all but filled with snow. The old frontiersman and the two youths took themselves into the woods where the snow was not so deep, and there presently came upon the tracks of some big animal which Barringford declared must be an elk.

"Let us get him by all means!" cried Henry, enthusiastically.

The others were willing enough, and followed the tracks of the elk a distance of quarter of a mile. Here they came to something of a buffalo trail, and were surprised to behold the prints of many feet and of snowshoes.

"Sam, what does this mean?" demanded Dave, quickly.

The old frontiersmen did not answer at once, but examined the prints with care. Then he brought his teeth together with a snap—a sure sign that he had made an important discovery.

"Injuns!" he said, laconically. "Injuns!"

"Indians!"

"Aye, lad—twenty or more on 'em, too,—an' headed up along close to the trail we made this morning."

"They must be following us," broke in Henry.

"It looks like it."

"Do you think they mean to attack us, Sam?" questioned Dave.

"They will ef they git the chanct, Dave. It ain't in human nature fer 'em not to—thet is, if they be enemies."

"They might be friends."

"Wall, I wouldn't gamble on thet, out here."

"What had we best do?"

"You an' Henry can go back and tell Mr. Morris about it. I'll go on an' do a little scout work."

So it was decided, and in a very few minutes Dave and Henry were on their way to the spot where the expedition had encamped. Sam Barringford followed the trail of the Indians, moving along with the secrecy that years of experience had given him.

"We must lose no time in getting back to camp," said Henry, as he and his cousin hurried along. "Every moment may be precious."

"Right you are, Henry. Oh, I hope we escape!"

"Captain Ecuyer must have been right—we have been watched."

Their hurried entrance into camp created some consternation, and the story they had to tell made every one uneasy. A council of war was held, and the camp was moved to another spot, where the frontiersmen might make a better stand, in case of an attack.

Two anxious hours went by, and all looked for the return of Sam Barringford, but he did not come. Then it began to grow dark, and guards were posted all around the camp, to give the alarm at the first appearance of any Indians.

Dave was on guard duty, close to some rocks which the wind had swept clear of snow, when he saw a figure stealing across an open glade a short distance away. Hardly had the figure appeared when two Indians came into view, each with a bow and arrows. Both red men aimed at the other figure and sent an arrow on its way. The figure threw up its arms and pitched headlong in the snow, beside a clump of bushes.

"It must be Sam Barringford!" cried the youth, to himself. "Sam—and he has been shot!"

It was an awful thought, and for the moment Dave did not know what to do. Then, as the Indians came closer, he took aim at one with his rifle and blazed away. The Indian staggered and fell, and then dragged himself back from the direction he had come, seriously wounded. The second Indian ran away and was quickly lost to view in the tall timber.

Dave was busy reloading, when his uncle rushed up, followed by two frontiersmen, all with their rifles in readiness to resist an attack.

"What was it, Dave?" questioned his uncle. And when told, he added: "Was it Sam?"

"I think so. He dropped——There he is now!"

As the youth uttered the words the man who had fallen picked himself up in a dazed way. He walked a few paces in one direction and then turned and walked in another. Clearly he did not know what he was doing.

"He has been struck and is hurt," said Joseph Morris. "Hello, come this way!" he called out. "Come this way!"

The man at first paid no attention, but presently he came towards them, reeling and staggering from weakness. One arrow was sticking through his arm, and the second had grazed the back of his head.

"Save me!" he moaned. "Don't let the—them ki—kill me!"

"We'll do what we can for you," answered Joseph Morris, and ran to take the man by the arm. He was an utter stranger, tall and slim, with curly black hair and dark eyes. His clothing had once been of the best, but was now much soiled and in rags.

"The Indians—they are all coming!" gasped the man, when he felt able to speak once more. "They have plotted to fall upon a pack-train bound for th—the we—west. I was their prisoner and thought to—to get to the pack-train and warn them of——" He tried to go on, but could not, and sank a leaden weight in Joseph Morris's arms.

"Poor fellow, he is almost done for," said one of the frontiersmen. "I don't think he will live."

"Let us carry him into camp," answered Joseph Morris. "He may not be so badly hurt as you think."

The two frontiersmen who had come up with Mr. Morris picked the senseless form up and hurried to the camp with it, where they did what they could for the sufferer. In the meantime Joseph Morris did a little scouting around, but could see nothing more of the Indians.

"The alarm has frightened them off for the time being," said Mr. Morris. "They may be too cowardly to attack us while we are wide-awake and on the watch."

Fortunately for the whites, the night proved to be an exceptionally clear one, with the stars glittering in the heavens like so many diamonds. It was quiet, saving for the far-away howls of some wolves and the occasional bark of a fox or hoot of an owl. But the frontiersmen kept on guard, not knowing what each succeeding minute might bring forth.

The man who had been brought in still lay unconscious and breathing heavily. He was a handsome individual, all of forty years of age, and evidently of good breeding. His face was pale, as if he had suffered much during his captivity among the Indians.

"I wish he was well enough to tell his tale," said Henry. "He might relate something to our advantage."

As the hours slipped by all the Morrises became anxious over the prolonged absence of Sam Barringford. At the most they had not expected the old frontiersman to remain away later than midnight.

"Perhaps something has happened to him," said Henry. "Those Indians are mighty slick."

"Oh, don't say that!" cried Dave. "Sam knew exactly what he was doing, and he ought to be able to take care of himself."

"He may have walked into some trap. You must remember, Dave, that some of the redskins out here are slyer than those in the East. They are regular foxes on the warpath."

Slowly the night wore away, until a glow in the east announced the coming of another day. The man who had been brought in was now conscious, but so weak he could scarcely speak. He wanted to tell them something, but could not, and sank back again utterly exhausted.

"Take it easy," said Joseph Morris, kindly. "We will do what we can for you." And at this, the man tried to smile, but it was a dismal failure.

"Tell me one thing," said Dave, who had come up a moment before. "Did you meet another white man in the woods—a frontiersman, one of our men?"

At this the man shook his head. "Nobody—on—only Indians!" he gasped.

"Then something has certainly happened to Sam," said Dave, and gave a sigh that came from the very bottom of his young heart.

CHAPTER XXIV
SNOWBOUND ON THE TRAIL

Another council of war was held, and two of the frontiersmen went scouting around once more. Not a sign was to be seen of the Indians, and at last Joseph Morris concluded to advance as before, but with everybody on the alert.

"If Sam comes back to this point he will know that we have gone on and can follow us up," said the planter.

The sick man had to be carried on a stretcher, and the men took turns at the task. As soon as breakfast was had, the expedition moved, three frontiersmen well to the front, on the watch for the first sign of the enemy.

Thus a mile had been covered, and they were approaching a spot where their route lay between a cliff and a hill, when an interruption came from the rear. The expedition halted, and a minute later Sam Barringford came up on a run, and well-nigh exhausted.

"I war afraid ye'd move afore I got back," panted the old frontiersman. "Ye hadn't ought to have done it. You be a-walkin' right into a hornets' nest."

"Where have you been?" questioned Dave.

"Been follerin' them Injuns. They are a bad crowd under Eagle Nose, an' they mean to wipe us out, if they kin do it. They held a grand pow-wow last night, and they have moved forward to the cliff and the hill thet's ahead. When we go through below they reckoned to shoot us down with bullets an' arrows, an' roll some big rocks down on us. I waited to learn jest what they war up to an' thet kept me from gittin' back to camp afore."

Sam Barringford, after that, related his night's adventures in detail. At no time had the Indians seen him or suspected his presence, and he had been so close that he had even stolen a gun belonging to one of them, a weapon of ancient French make, which he now had with him.

Having no desire to run into the "hornets' nest" which the old frontiersman had described, Joseph Morris determined to move onward by another route. This suited Barringford, but he was of a mind to attack the Indians because of the plot they had concocted.

"We must teach 'em a lesson," he said. "If we don't, it won't be safe travelin' for us at any time."

This was considered sound advice by many present, and in the end it was decided that six men should climb the hill ahead, coming out above the Indians if possible. The rest of the expedition, in the meantime, was to move onward around the cliff, making a wide detour, to avoid all possible contact with the enemy.

"I want to go with Sam," said Henry to his father, and was at last permitted to accompany the old frontiersman. Dave had to remain with the others, to help take care of the horses and the sick man.

Sam Barringford knew exactly where he was going, having traveled the ground several times in the past. He was a natural-born woodsman, and never forgot a locality once he had visited it. To him trees and rocks were the same as signboards to a dweller in the city. The only time he got lost was when a territory was entirely new to him.

The way was by no means an easy one and, when the top of the hill was reached, the tramp through the snow had taken the wind out of more than one of the detachment. The men and Henry rested for a few minutes, and then, cautioned by Barringford, moved slowly and cautiously over the hilltop in the direction of the trail far below.

"Halt!" whispered Sam Barringford, presently. "I see an Injun!" And he pointed out the red warrior two hundred feet or more below them.

The Indian was watching the trail below, and soon he was joined by ten or a dozen others. The Indians were totally unconscious of the fact that some white men were looking down upon them, and their eyes were fixed steadfastly upon the trail below, watching for the first appearance of the Morris expedition.

"What a trap!" murmured Henry. "Had we been caught in it, nothing could have saved us."

"Right you are, Henry," said another of the party. "Sam deserves a good deal of credit for saving us."

To give the others of the expedition time to get as far as possible from the scene of action, it was decided to wait awhile before beginning an attack on the Indians. The latter waited patiently for over an hour, when they began to show some uneasiness, thinking their plot had miscarried.

"Now we'll show 'em a trick or two," said Sam Barringford, and gave the order to advance.

The Indians were taken completely by surprise, and at the first fire of the English three fell, one dead and the others mortally wounded. One other was struck in the thigh and rolled down the hill on to the trail below.

"Give it to 'em again!" roared Sam Barringford. "Give it to 'em, the sons o' Satan!" And he fired a second time, while some of the others did the same. Another Indian went down, and then the rest fled, in several directions. The whites went after them, and in the end fully half of the band under Eagle Nose were exterminated. Eagle Nose himself was struck in the left forearm, and withdrew with the rest of his warriors, vowing bitter vengeance.

Of the whites, strange to state, not one was injured, although the red men fired arrows and shots at them many times. One arrow went through the hunting shirt of one of the frontiersmen, and a bullet clipped the cap of another, and that was all. The Indians fled to the northward, and that was the last seen of them for a long while to come. Some were very bitter against Eagle Nose for leading them into a trap, as they expressed it, and there was some talk of deposing the chief, but nothing came of this.

"Sam, you saved us from utter annihilation," said Joseph Morris, when the two parts of the expedition had been once more united. "I thank you from the bottom of my heart," and he gave the old frontiersman's hand a tight squeeze.

"I wish I had been in that fight," said Dave to Henry. "It must have been exciting."

"It was, but not as much so as some of the fights we had during the war," answered his cousin. "We had the Indians on the run from the very start."

No time was now lost in moving forward, it being Joseph Morris's wish to leave the Indians as far behind as possible. They traveled until late at night, when they reached a safe shelter among the rocks and trees. It was now cloudy once more, and soon after they went into camp it began to snow.

"We are in for a heavy fall," said Dave, and he was right. The snow continued all night and all of the next day, and still there was no let-up to the storm. They remained in the temporary camp, watching the fall anxiously.

"Dave, I really believe we are going to be snowed in!" cried Henry, as he walked outside, to get a good look at the sky. "It doesn't seem to brighten up a bit!"

"Just what I am thinking," answered his cousin. "It is certainly coming down as thickly as ever."

All were now watching the snowfall, and they went to bed with anxious hearts. Dave woke up just at dawn. The snow had stopped, but there was more overhead, as he could easily see.

"If only this storm had kept off a few days longer," sighed Joseph Morris. Three days of fair traveling would have brought the expedition to the vicinity of the trading post.

Breakfast was had, and all were wondering if they could make any headway in such a depth of snow when the flakes began to come down again. The whole landscape was blotted out in a sea of whirling flakes.

"That settles it; we remain here," grumbled Dave. The nearer he drew to the trading post the more anxious he became to learn the whole truth of the situation there.

The men of the expedition made themselves as comfortable as possible, and not to be caught without provisions, some went out on a short hunt. They managed to bring down a few birds, but that was all—not worth the powder and shot, as Barringford declared.

Dave was greatly interested in the sick man, who dozed away the greater portion of the time. Once or twice the youth tried to engage the man in conversation, but the effort was a failure.

"I'll have to wait till he feels more like himself," said Dave to Henry. "One thing is certain, he is not used to a life in the open or used to roughing it in any way."

"It is queer how he came among the Indians, Dave. He will most likely have quite a story to tell—if he is ever able to tell it."

"Oh, I think he will recover, don't you?"

"Yes, physically, but——" And Henry shrugged his shoulders.

"You think it will affect him here?" And Dave tapped his forehead.

"Perhaps. Don't you remember Dick Barsbee? He went crazy from the Indian tortures he endured."

"Yes, I remember that." Dave shook his head. "I hope the man comes around all right. I must say there is something about him that interests me a great deal."

"Does his face look familiar to you?"

"It certainly does,—but I can't trace the likeness to save myself."

"It's the same way with me, and Sam Barringford says the same. Now what can it mean?"

"We may find out when we learn who the man is."

The snow continued all of that day and far into the night. Then the wind arose, sweeping great drifts of white across the landscape. The expedition was under the shelter of a cliff and some trees, and was snowed in beyond a doubt.

"Snowbound!" cried Sam Barringford, grimly. "Here we be an' here we are likely to stay fer some time to come."

"We are certainly shut in pretty well," returned Joseph Morris. "At the best, we'll have to dig our way out."

"The hosses could never git through on the trail," put in one of the frontiersmen. "It would be cruelty to try it. Why, the snow must be ten an' twelve feet deep in some o' the hollows."

"And we'd lose our way," said another. "Might as well stay where we are and be comfortable until it clears a bit." He was troubled with soreness of the feet, and found traveling very hard.

"We can't stay here very long," said Joseph Morris. "We have lost so much time our provisions are running low."

The matter was discussed for an hour, and they decided to remain in the camp and make themselves as comfortable as possible. The snow was banked up for shelter, and pine boughs cut for couches, and a roaring fire was kept going all the while.

"It's a pity we must stay here," sighed Dave. "I think if we could reach the post in such weather as this we would take Jean Bevoir and his crowd completely by surprise."

"I think so myself," replied Henry. "But we must be patient, and take matters as they come."

CHAPTER XXV
CRUSHING NEWS

The expedition had to remain in camp for the best part of a week, and during that time provisions ran exceedingly low. To stock the larder several of the men, and also Dave and Henry, went out in the near-by woods and shot whatever came into sight. The two youths were fortunate in bringing down several wild turkeys of good size and also uncovered a sleeping bear that they killed with ease. This meat came in when the stock of provisions was at its lowest, and proved highly acceptable.

At last the trail seemed to be fit to use once more, and Joseph Morris ordered the advance to be made. It was hard walking, either on foot or on snowshoes, and many times the poor horses refused to go another step and had to rest for an hour at a time. Six miles were all they could cover the first day after starting, and the youths felt as tired as if they had walked five times that distance. Moving the sick stranger was a harder task than ever, but nobody thought of leaving him behind.

The second day, however, brought an improvement. They gained a small creek flowing into the Kinotah and followed this to the larger stream. Walking on the ice was easier than in the snow. Occasionally one or another would slip down, but nobody complained.

"We are at the old post!" cried Dave, as the burnt district came into view. They stopped for dinner on the spot, and then took their way down the Kinotah to the Ohio.

The weather was now moderating rapidly, so that during the middle of the day the sun was positively warm. Much of the snow turned to slush and water, freezing a little at night and thawing more than ever during the day. The surface of the river became wet, and Joseph Morris cautioned all against stepping on ice that might be rotten.

"If this weather keeps on it won't be long before there is a spring freshet," remarked Sam Barringford. "Queer how quickly things change in nature."

"That big snowfall about wound up the winter," answered Henry, and he was right, as it afterwards proved.

It was Joseph Morris's plan to halt when about a mile from the trading post and then go forward with Sam Barringford and one or two others and reconnoiter the situation. As the expedition neared the post all kept on the alert for the possible appearance of Bevoir or any of his crowd.

"For all we know Moon Eye may not be in the post at all, but somewhere on the outside, on guard," said Dave, who accompanied his uncle and Barringford when reconnoitering.

Mr. Morris, Barringford, and Dave advanced with extreme caution. It was another warm day, with the sun shining brightly and the snow melting rapidly on all sides. They kept among the bushes and trees until they came to a point where they could see a corner of the stockade plainly.

"Do you see anybody around?" asked Dave. He was so agitated that he could not speak. Oh, if only he knew the whole truth about his father!

Sam Barringford shook his head and so did Joseph Morris. Not a soul could be seen, and slowly the three made their way to a point opposite the stockade gate.

"The gate is shut," announced Dave. "I suppose it is barred, too."

"More'n likely," answered Sam Barringford. He was looking at the loopholes with a critical eye. "They are on guard," he announced, a minute later.

"How do you know that?" questioned Joseph Morris.

"Saw a feller squinting through a loophole jest now. Thar's another!" went on the old frontiersman.

"I see an Indian!" said Dave, and pointed along the stockade, where a crack in the posts had given him a glimpse of some feathers. "They are surely on the watch."

"Then they must have learned of our coming!" murmured the planter, and was much discouraged.

A thorough survey of the situation convinced them that the party at the post was indeed on guard. The alarm had been given by a runner of Eagle Nose's tribe, who had brought the word for Moon Eye's benefit, the latter chief being related to him by marriage. Jean Bevoir had been greatly surprised, but had at once issued orders both to the Frenchmen and the Indians to keep a close guard.

"Ve shall fight zem," he said, boldly. "Fight zem to ze end! I vill show zem zat za cannot stand against Jean Bevoir!"

The Frenchman had procured a good stock of rifles and ammunition, and everybody in the post was, consequently, well armed. More than this, the palisade had been strengthened at various points, making the trading post a veritable fortress.

The runner had not told Bevoir or Moon Eye how many men there were with Joseph Morris, but said there must be at least a dozen. In the post were now assembled ten Frenchmen, several of whom had been soldiers in the army during the war for the possession of Canada, and fourteen Indians under Moon Eye. There were also three Indian women and five Indian children—all that were left of the tribe since the downfall of Pontiac's conspiracy.

What to do next was a problem hard for Joseph Morris to solve. The more he surveyed the situation the more he became convinced that to attack the post openly would prove highly disastrous.

"They have the best of the situation," said he to Dave and the others. "They could pick us off through the loopholes at will. Perhaps I had better parley with them."

"Ye can't parley with Bevoir," answered Sam Barringford, in disgust.

"And why not?"

"Because ye can't believe a word the Frencher says. Thet man would rather lie nor eat."

"But perhaps I can convince him that he cannot hold the post," went on the planter.

"Well, ye kin do as ye please, Mr. Morris, but I don't agree to it. Ye don't know the varmint as I do, an' as Mr. James Morris did,—an' as Dave an' Henry do. We have got to git the best o' them, either in the open or by trickery. He won't listen to reason until he's licked good an' proper."

"I think Sam is right," said Dave, as his uncle looked at him. "Jean Bevoir is not to be trusted—father and I found that out a number of times, to our sorrow. He may promise all sorts of things,—but he won't keep his word unless it suits him to do so."

Nevertheless, rather than risk a fight at the beginning, Joseph Morris resolved to have a talk with the French trader, and for that purpose sent a frontiersman named Hope to the post. Hope carried a white handkerchief tied to a stick, and was allowed to come to within a few paces of the stockade gate, when he was halted.

"I want to talk to Jean Bevoir," said the frontiersman.

"Vat you vant?" demanded the Frenchman, from within, and without showing himself.

"Is that you, Jean Bevoir?"

"Yees."

"Joseph Morris is here with a large party, and he demands that you throw the gate of this post open."

"Ha! Vat for, tell me zat? So he can come in and murder us, not so?"

"If you will not open the gate and let him march in he will come in by force."

"Let heem try it! Let heem try it!" cried Jean Bevoir, in a rage. "Zis is my post—I vill defend my property. Now I vant you to go avay—an' stay avay!" he added, sharply.

"Will you talk to Mr. Morris?"

"Vy I do zat? Haf I not told you vat to do? Go avay!"

"He has something of great importance to say to you. Perhaps he will make terms," continued Hope, wishing to bring the two men together, so that he might not have too much responsibility on his own shoulders.

Jean Bevoir demurred and was evidently seconded by some other Frenchmen within the post, but at last he consented to talk to Joseph Morris, provided the planter would come to the gate unattended. Secretly the French trader was anxious to know just what the English had in mind to do.

Hope went back and delivered his message. At once Dave, Henry, and Barringford set up another protest.

"There is sure to be treachery, father!" cried Henry. "Why, they may even shoot you down in cold blood. You do not know the temper of these black-hearted rascals."

"I do not think they will dare to go as far as that," answered Joseph Morris. He was brave-hearted to the core. "If they do kill me attack them and show no mercy," he added.

The conference between Jean Bevoir and the planter took place an hour later. Joseph Morris, waving a white handkerchief, approached the front of the trading post boldly. He saw himself covered by several rifle barrels, but did not falter. As he came to a halt there was a slight noise, as a short ladder was thrown into place, and then the head of Jean Bevoir appeared over the stockade gate.

"Hullo! Jean Bevoir has shown himself!" cried Dave, who was at a distance. "I must say, I didn't think he would do it."

"He wants us to believe that he is not afraid," answered Henry. "Probably he has been fortifying his courage with a few drinks of rum." And in this guess Henry hit the nail on the head.

"Jean Bevoir," began James Morris. "Do you realize that you have committed a great wrong?"

"I haf done no wrong," returned the Frenchman, stubbornly. "This post ees mine; I shall keep heem."

"You killed my brother."

"It ees not so,—I did not touch heem."

"But he is dead, is not that true?" demanded the planter, with a sudden hope swaying in his heart.

"Yees, he ees dead. But I did it not, no. An Indian shot heem down—who, I know not. He vas badly wounded, an' I, yes, I hees enemy, took care of heem, *oui*, until he died. Zen I gif heem a good burial. Vat can I do more? He not do so much for Jean Bevoir, no! no!"

"You caused his death—the attack on him and his companions was your work,—it is useless to deny it. And this post is not yours. Since my brother is dead it belongs to his son, David Morris,—and he shall have it, be the cost what it may. Jean Bevoir, you must surrender, or take the consequences."

At this plain speech the Frenchman grew slightly pale. But he quickly recovered.

"Ha! Take care how you threaten Jean Bevoir!" he exclaimed. "Ve are vell armed here an' ve can shoot! Haf I not told you zat zis post ees mine? I haf ze papers, wid ze signature of James Morris, *oui*! Ze law ees as good for me as for you, an' I snap my fingair at you!" Jean Bevoir suited the action to the word. "Go avay, an' nevair come here again!"

"You have my brother's signature? Impossible! It must be a forgery! He would never deal in that way with such as you."

"Eet ees true, an' I warn you avay. Come back again at your peril!" answered Jean Bevoir, and then disappeared from view.

This was a signal that the conference was at an end. Turning swiftly, Joseph Morris walked back into the forest. Barringford and the others expected a shot or two, but nothing of the kind came.

"What did he say?" asked Henry, rushing up.

"He will give in to nothing," answered the planter, with a sigh.

"And father—what of father?" questioned Dave. He could hardly utter the words.

James Morris stepped to his side and caught Dave by both arms.

"It's too bad, my boy," he said, tenderly.

"Then he is—is———"

"Yes, lad—he was badly wounded, so Jean Bevoir says, and died some time later."

Dave staggered and sank down on a fallen tree. Never had he felt so miserable before. For days and weeks he had been hoping against hope—and now it had all been in vain. His father was gone, and he was left alone in the world.

CHAPTER XXVI
BY WAY OF THE TUNNEL

"There is one consolation: if we cannot get into the post they cannot very well get out. If the worst comes to the worst maybe we can starve them into submission,"

Henry uttered the words after a long council of war between his father and the other men of the expedition. All had withdrawn to the shelter of the forest, and were keeping a close watch on the trading post.

Dave took but little interest in what was said. He was thinking of the loss of his father. It was a terrible blow, and he did not see how he would ever get over it.

"Your plan is all right, Henry, but it would take too long," said Sam Barringford. "More'n likely Bevoir an' his crowd have a good stock o' rations on hand an' kin hold out all winter. They have shelter while we have none. I've got another plan, although it's mighty risky. Don't ye remember thet tunnel from the yard out into this forest? If the rascals ain't discovered thet we might use it in the dark an' git into the post thet way."

"Yes! yes!" cried Henry, brightening. "The tunnel Tony Jadwin and I used. It came out in a hollow tree only a short distance from here. I am sure I can find the tree easily enough."

"It is more than likely they have found the tunnel," answered Joseph Morris. "And if so, they will watch it, or block it up."

"I'm a-goin' to take a look," said the old frontiersman.

While the majority of the men continued to watch the trading post, to guard against a possible attack by those inside, the planter, Barringford, Henry, and Dave walked to the hollow tree. How this was used before has already been told in another volume of this series.

It was an easy matter for Sam Barringford to let himself down into the hollow tree. He had to clear away a little snow, but found the tunnel practically empty. It was only a small affair, dug for bitter emergency, and ran directly from the hollow tree under the palisade, and came out near a corner of the storehouse. It had several turns, around rocks and roots of trees long since cut down, and it took some time for the old frontiersman to worm his way along until he reached the vicinity of its termination.

To light his way, Barringford had brought along a small torch, and now he stuck this behind him, in the wall of the tunnel. In front of him was a large flat stone, covering the end of the passageway.

He placed his ear to the stone and listened. Not a sound broke the stillness beyond, and gently but firmly he pushed on one end of the stone. It was frozen fast, but at last came away, letting down a small shower of snow.

"Covered with snow, eh?" he murmured to himself. "So much the better. They ain't found it, an' more'n likely they don't know a thing about it."

With extreme caution he continued to push upon the stone, until he had raised up one end a foot or more. Beyond, he now discovered a drift of snow, covered with an icy crust. All he had to do was to clear away the snow, break the crust, and step out into the open, less than ten feet away from the door to the storehouse and stable.

Not deeming it wise to go further in the daylight, Barringford allowed the stone to drop into place once more, and wormed his way back to the hollow tree. The others were anxiously awaiting his return.

"What did you find?" asked Henry.

"We can git in that way, if we want to," answered the old frontiersman, and related the particulars.

Dave was for entering the post at once, but Joseph Morris shook his head, and Barringford did the same.

"We had better wait until nightfall," said the planter, "and in the meantime perhaps we can throw Jean Bevoir off his guard."

"Let us pretend to go away," said Henry. "Have a talk with him, and say you will come back with a company of regulars from Fort Pitt."

This was considered a good suggestion, and a little later Joseph Morris walked again into the open, waving his white handkerchief. At first nobody paid attention to him. Then Bevoir showed himself once more.

"Jean Bevoir, we have talked matters over," began the planter. "We want you to consider well before you decide. Will you give up the post, or do you want us to return to Fort Pitt and bring a company of soldiers here to fight you?"

"I vill not give up ze post, no!" shouted the French trader.

"Then you want us to bring the soldiers from Fort Pitt?"

"You cannot do zat," was the reply, but a look of anxiety crossed the bronzed features of the French rascal.

"I think I can do it. Captain Ecuyer is my friend, and was the friend of my brother. He will aid us all he can."

"Ze post ees mine, haf I not said so before? Ze *capitaine* must respect Jean Bevoir's rights. Ven he comes here I show heem ze papairs. He must respect ze document, *oui.*"

"You have no right to this place, and I know it," answered Joseph Morris, doggedly. "Then you will not give up?"

"No, nevair!"

"Then, when we bring the soldiers, the consequence be on your own head," said the trader, and walked away to join his friends. He was just entering the forest when a rifle shot rang out and the bullet whistled close to his ear.

"The skunks!" roared Sam Barringford. "Didn't I tell ye they wasn't to be trusted?"

"I think I have fooled them," said the planter. The shot had somewhat disturbed him, but he did not show it. "Now, let us pretend to break camp and march away."

This was done with great skillfulness, at a point where those in the post could see what was going on. Everything was packed on the horses and they moved off, up the Ohio. They continued to journey onward until darkness and a bend in the river hid them from the view of their enemy.

"Now to get back, and get ready for the attack," said Joseph Morris, and he had Barringford lead the way, by a route deep in the forest, where it would be impossible for anybody at the post to catch sight of them.

The marching away of the expedition was viewed with interest by Jean Bevoir, Moon Eye, and their followers. At first they imagined it might be a ruse, but then concluded that Joseph Morris really intended to go to Fort Pitt for assistance.

"What he said about Captain Ecuyer is true," said Benoit Vascal to Jean Bevoir, in their own tongue. "The Morrises were warm friends of the fort commandant. He will surely do all he can for them."

"The soldiers will aid their own," said Moon Eye. "Did not these whites get aid when Moon Eye was fighting them? If they reach Fort Pitt and obtain assistance it may go hard with all of us."

"It is a long journey," said Jean Bevoir.

"Yes, but spring is at hand," answered Moon Eye. "Soon the trail will be open, and then the journey will not be difficult. The soldiers will be glad of a march, after being housed up so long."

"And what do you advise?" asked the French trader.

"Let us follow them on the sly and shoot them down. They will not dream of our leaving the post. We can fall upon them when they are asleep and kill them to a man."

"Yes! yes! let us do that!" said a warrior who was eager for bloodshed. "Remember the saying, 'the dead bear brings no news to her cubs.'"

A general council of war was held, and the upshot of the matter was that it was decided to leave the post under the care of two of the Frenchmen and two Indians. All of the others, including Moon Eye, Jean Bevoir, and Benoit Vascal, prepared to follow up the Morris expedition as soon as it seemed safe to do so.

Unconscious of what was in the minds of their enemy, our friends made a long detour through the mighty forest and arrived in the vicinity of the post once more shortly after midnight. They found everything remarkably quiet and not a single light of any kind was showing.

Barringford lost no time in entering the tunnel, followed by Dave and Henry. The others came after, each taking his gun and hunting knife with him.

"Be cautious," warned Joseph Morris. "Do not risk a shot needlessly."

When the old frontiersman reached the flat stone he shoved it up as before. All was still quiet and dark, and scraping away some of the snow he broke the icy covering and peered forth. He could see the storehouse and stable and above was the clear sky, with the stars twinkling far overhead.

"Nobuddy in sight," he whispered, after a careful survey of the surroundings.

He stepped out of the tunnel and like a ghost vanished into a dark angle of the storehouse building. Dave and Henry followed him, and then came Joseph Morris and some others.

The hearts of all beat rapidly, for they felt that they were taking their lives in their hands. A discovery might mean death for many and perhaps all of them.

"Ha! I see a man!" whispered Barringford, and pointed out a Frenchman, stationed, gun in hand, near the stockade gate.

"And there is an Indian," put in Dave, pointing to another portion of the post defense.

Try their best they could see no others on guard. The Frenchman and the Indian walked up and down slowly, stopping every few minutes to peer through one loophole or another.

"The others must be asleep," whispered Joseph Morris. "If so we may be able to surprise them completely."

In a few minutes all of the party were out of the tunnel. Several looked into the stable and storehouse, to find both empty, saving for stores, pelts, and horses.

"Let us move to the main building," whispered Joseph Morris. "At the first sign of an outbreak, fire on them and show them no quarter."

"They need expect no quarter from me, Jean Bevoir especially," answered Dave, grimly.

The entrance to the main building was gained, and still they caught sight of nobody but the two guards near the stockade. Softly the door was pushed open and Sam Barringford entered, followed by Joseph Morris and Dave and Henry.

A bright fire burnt in the big open chimney, casting a ruddy glare around the room. In front of the fire, on the floor, lay an Indian, snoring lustily. On a couch in a corner rested a Frenchman, also asleep.

Without awaking the sleepers, Dave and Henry glided into the sleeping room of the post. Here it was dark, and they had to go slow, for fear of arousing somebody. They felt their way from bunk to bunk, listening intently and putting forth cautious hands. Then they tiptoed their way back to the main room.

"The bunks are empty!" whispered Dave, and Henry nodded.

"All of them?" queried Joseph Morris.

"Yes."

"They must be outside—maybe they are going to trap us after all," came softly from Sam Barringford. "We had better——"

He stopped short and raised his long rifle. The sleeping Frenchman had roused up and was staring at the intruders. He rubbed his eyes in bewilderment.

"What want you here?" he stammered, in French.

"Silence!" came sternly from the old frontiersman. "Silence, ef ye don't want to be kilt!"

The Frenchman understood little of English, but he understood enough, and he calmly submitted to being bound with a rope that was handy. In the midst of the work the Indian awoke, gave a swift look around, and started for the doorway, uttering a war-cry as he did so.

"Stop!" cried Joseph Morris, and fired his rifle at the red warrior. His aim was true, and the Indian went down, wounded in the back. Then came a shout from outside in French, followed by a war-whoop.

"We must fight for it now!" cried Henry.

"I am ready!" answered Dave. "Come on! The quicker we get at them the better!"

CHAPTER XXVII
HOLDING THE TRADING POST

All ran out of the main building, looking in every direction for the enemy. They expected to be confronted by at least a dozen Frenchmen and Indians, and when these did not appear James Morris and his followers were much perplexed.

The Indian at the stockade fired on them, and so did the Frenchman at the gate. Our friends fired in return, and the Frenchman went down with two bullets in his breast. The Indian was slightly wounded, and as he saw the others pouring from the main building, he turned back to the stockade, ran to one of the corners, climbed up and over, and disappeared from view.

"He is running away!" cried Dave. "Something is wrong here! Where can Jean Bevoir be?"

Nobody attempted to answer that question, just then. The party scattered throughout the grounds and the buildings, looking in all directions for the enemy. But nobody was found outside of those already seen.

"They have disappeared," said Joseph Morris. "Can it be possible that they have gone out to follow us up?"

"That's it!" shouted Henry. "They didn't want us to go to Fort Pitt for aid."

"Henry must have hit the truth," said Sam Barringford. "It's a lucky thing fer us. We have gained the post with no loss at all."

"But it remains to be seen if we can hold it," answered Joseph Morris, quickly.

"Don't forget that Indian who got away," added Dave. "He will carry the news to the others as soon as he can, and they will be about our ears in no time."

"We must prepare to defend this place," said his uncle. "I will call the men together, and we can go over our plans. Dave, you know more of this post than I do. How had we best distribute the men?"

Dave told of what had been done in the past, and soon the men were put on guard, two at the gate, one at each corner of the stockade, and the others at a point in the center of the grounds, from which they could run to any spot where they were needed. Each man was armed with two rifles, and some of them had a pistol besides,—old Spanish weapons and extra long.

"We must not forget that our horses are still in the forest and likewise that sick man," said Joseph Morris. "If possible, we ought to bring them in."

"If you say so, I'll go after them," answered his son. "I am not afraid to do it."

At first the planter demurred, but finally consented to let Henry go, accompanied by Sam Barringford. They did not wish their pack-train to fall into the hands of Bevoir and Moon Eye, for that would give the enemy a great advantage. Besides, they felt it their duty to care for the stranger who had sought their aid.

"You must return with all possible speed," said Joseph Morris, when Henry and Barringford were departing. "If you hurry you will likely get back before Jean Bevoir starts to return to this post."

The two departed by climbing the stockade at one of the corners, and lost not a moment in getting into the shelter of the timber. Here they looked around carefully, but could not find a single trace of their enemy or of the Indian who had vanished.

The Indian who had been wounded in the short fight at the post refused to speak when questioned. Dave recognized him as one of Moon Eye's followers whom he had met before. When the red warrior saw the youth he merely scowled and turned his face away. A little later he lapsed into unconsciousness, and nobody paid further attention to him, thinking he was about to breathe his last.

The Frenchman who had been captured was a man Henry and Barringford had met several times. He was a lawless and brutal fellow, given to heavy drinking, and he took his capture with an air of bravo and told them to do their worst if they chose.

"What has become of Jean Bevoir?" asked Mr. Morris of the man.

"Jean, he ees ze big fool," was the answer. "He go to catch you—you come here an' tak post. By gar! dat ees big fool t'ing!"

"Tell me about my father," said Dave. "How was he wounded and how did he die?"

"Vat I know 'bout dat? I no keel heem! I no see heem 't all. Jean, he fix dat, I tell you!" And the Frenchman winked suggestively.

"I suppose you mean that Bevoir killed my father," went on Dave, bitterly.

"I no say dat, no. You ask Jean—he tell truth—I haf noddings to do wid dat, no!" And then the Frenchman would say no more on the subject, nor would he say what had become of the others who had accompanied James Morris. Evidently he did not wish to render himself liable in any manner if it could be avoided.

Slowly the night wore away and morning dawned, bright and clear. To the chagrin of those at the post neither Henry nor Barringford showed himself, nor did they see anything of the sick man or the horses.

"I hope they have not gotten into trouble," said Joseph Morris. "Yet, if all went well, they should have been here long before this."

It was about nine o'clock in the morning when they heard several shots at a distance. They watched eagerly, and presently saw Sam Barringford, on horseback, riding with might and main for the post.

"Sam is coming!" cried Dave, running to the gate. "Put down the bars and let him in!"

The bars were loosened and the big gate opened, and a minute later the old frontiersman swept through the opening. He was so exhausted he almost dropped from his steed.

"Is Henry here?" were his first words.

"No," answered several.

At this announcement the face of the frontiersman fell. He glanced back toward the forest.

"It's too bad, but we can't do nuthing now. Bar the gate ag'in, afore they git in on ye!"

His directions were followed, and soon after this the party under Jean Bevoir and Moon Eye swept into view. They were in a great rage, and doubly so when they saw how they had been tricked out of the possession of the trading post.

The old frontiersman swept through the opening.

"Surrendair!" cried Jean Bevoir, as he came closer. "Zat ees my property, an' I call upon you to surrendair!"

"Keep your distance, or we will fire upon you!" answered Joseph Morris, and to check the advance he had one of his men fire over the enemy's head. At this the advancing party lost no time in secreting itself behind the neighboring trees.

"Keep a strict watch and sound the alarm at the first outbreak," said the planter, and then walked to where Dave was assisting Sam Barringford from his steed.

The frontiersman's story was soon told. He and Henry had gone straight to where the pack-train and the sick man had been left, to find the man gone and also one of the horses. They were looking around for the individual and the steed when five Indians pounced upon them and made them prisoners. The Indians took them into the forest and also led the horses away. From their talk they were evidently a portion of Moon Eye's tribe that was journeying to the post to join their chief. What had become of the sick man none of them appeared to know.

"We watched our chances," continued Sam Barringford, "and jest when we thought as how we could do it, Henry an' I made a break fer liberty. We got on two o' the hosses an' rode as if the Old Nick war after us. The Injuns fired at us, but their aim was no good so far ez I was consarned. In the woods Henry an' I got separated. I thought he rode straight fer here, but I must have been mistook on that p'int. I was coming along full bent when I spotted Jean Bevoir and Moon Eye and thet crowd. Then I knowed I must ride fer all I was wuth, an' I did it."

"Then Henry must be somewhere in the forest," said Dave.

"Yes, but if he's alive or dead I don't know," answered Sam Barringford, soberly.

"I must find out about this," said Joseph Morris. "And I must do it at once."

"You cannot go out now, Uncle Joe," said Dave, hastily. "They would shoot you on the spot!"

"No, ye can't go now," added Barringford.

A short time passed, and then came a hail from without. Looking they saw Jean Bevoir waving a bit of dirty white cloth.

"He wants another pow-wow," said a frontiersman at the gate.

"If I were you I'd not show myself," said Dave, to his uncle, but Joseph Morris mounted the short ladder nevertheless.

"What do you want now?" demanded the planter.

"I vish to make terms," began Jean Bevoir, and then went over his old story of his rights regarding the post.

"Jean Bevoir, I do not wish to listen to you," answered the planter. "This post belongs to David Morris, and that is the end of it. The best you can do is to take yourself off and be quick about it. All of this land now belongs to the English, and you Frenchmen have no rights here at all. If you want to establish a post you must do it in French territory. The war with your country and with the Indians is at an end, and you must act according to the treaty of peace. You are accountable for the death of my brother, and that is bad enough, without making matters worse. Go away, and never let me see your face again."

"I vill go—but I shall come back!" shouted Jean Bevoir, in a rage, and shaking his fist at Joseph Morris he retreated once more behind the trees.

"Did he say anything about Henry?" asked Dave.

"No. I will ask him," answered his uncle, and started to call to Jean Bevoir, when Barringford stopped him.

"Don't ye do it," said the old frontiersman. "Maybe they don't know Henry is still out, an' if so, it won't be wise to let 'em know."

"That is true," answered the planter, thoughtfully. "I will say nothing. But pray Heaven that my boy is safe!"

After that the best part of the day passed slowly. The only excitement occurred when the French prisoner broke his bonds and tried to escape. He was overtaken by one of the frontiersmen and a desperate hand-to-hand fight ensued, in which the frontiersman was stabbed in the shoulder. But then the Frenchman received a pistol bullet in his abdomen and fell flat. He was picked up and taken to the main building of the post, where he received such medical attention as the limited means of the garrison afforded. This did small good, however, and he died at sunrise on the following day. Before he died he tried to tell Dave something about James Morris, but couldn't speak clearly.

"What do you want to say?" asked Dave. "Tell me if you can."

"Your fadder, he ees—he ees——" said the wounded man, and that was as far as he could get. He gasped for breath, tried to sit up,—and a minute later all was over.

"He must have known something," said Dave, to his uncle. "What was it?"

The planter shook his head. "Do not ask me, Dave," he said, gently. "It is too bad! First your father, and now it may be Henry!" And he turned away to hide the tears that sprang into his eyes.

Dave could not content himself, and wandered idly from one part of the trading post to another. His father was continually in his mind. He missed his parent as he had never done before.

Suddenly as he walked along one of the men came running towards him.

"I say, Dave, have you seen that redskin that was wounded in the fight?" he called out. "The one your uncle shot?"

"No, I haven't seen him."

"He is gone—we can't find him anywhere. We all thought he was dying, but it looks now as if he had gotten away," went on the man.

He turned into the stable and then into a small compartment of the storehouse, where the powder for the post was usually kept. A moment later he came rushing into the open yelling wildly.

"The Injun's in there!" he gasped. "He has got a torch and is going to set off all the powder and blow us sky-high!"

CHAPTER XXVIII
IN WHICH A BATTERING RAM IS USED

The announcement that the frontiersman made filled Dave and the others who heard it with horror. For the moment the youth could not believe the evidence of his senses.

"Going to blow us up?" he queried.

"Yes—look for yourself, if you don't believe it!" And the man ran further away than ever.

"What does he say?" asked Joseph Morris, who had just come up.

"He says the Indian you wounded is in the storehouse and is going to set fire to the casks of powder stored there."

"In there?" returned the planter.

"Let us stop him—if we can," went on Dave, and rushed forward, without considering the great risk he was assuming by such action.

He ran into the storehouse, and his uncle came at his heels. Sure enough, the wounded Indian was there, firebrand in hand. He was waving it over a powder keg that was broken open and muttering a weird chant. He knew that he was mortally wounded, and if he had to die he wanted his hated enemies to die with him.

Dave and his uncle gazed on the scene as if bound by a spell. A single spark from that torch dropped into the powder would mean death and destruction to nearly everybody and everything in the post. The Indian was calm and continued to chant.

Presently, with a start, Dave broke the spell that bound him. He made one swift leap, caught the torch from behind and sent it whizzing away through the open doorway. Some sparks dropped to the floor and as they fell his foot covered them.

The Indian, taken completely off his guard, turned in consternation. The youth sprang upon him and bore him to the floor. Then Joseph Morris leaped in, and together they dragged the miscreant out of the building.

A crowd of half a dozen had collected. They saw the torch and saw the red man pushed and dragged into the open. They waited for an explosion, but it did not come. Then all began to breathe easier.

"Dave, you saved us all!" It was Joseph Morris who spoke. The great beads of perspiration were standing out on his forehead.

"I—I am glad if I did," answered the youth. Now the danger was past, he found himself trembling like a leaf.

"Kill that Injun!" was the cry. "Kill him! He ain't fit to live!"

Swiftly the crowd turned on the red man. The Indian had sunk on the ground in a heap. His wound had broken afresh and he was gasping heavily. Barringford ran to him, hunting knife in hand. Then the old frontiersman shook his head and motioned the others back.

"He's dying, men," he said. "Let him alone."

"Are ye sure o' thet, Sam?" asked one man.

"Dead sartin." And Barringford's words proved true, for the Indian expired soon after.

The alarm had put everybody in the post on his mettle, and a strict hunt was made, to see if anybody else was in hiding around the place. Nobody was found, and gradually the garrison settled down.

"It is maddening to think that Henry is missing," said Joseph Morris, shortly after the noon hour. "I would give a great deal to know what has become of him."

"And I'd like to know what Jean Bevoir intends to do next," returned his nephew.

"He and his followers may wait until to-night and then attack us."

Slowly the rest of the day wore away, and during that time all in the post made themselves as comfortable as possible. An examination of the stores showed that the Frenchmen and Indians had provided themselves with plenty of food, so the present garrison would not suffer in that respect.

"So far as rations are concerned, we can hold this place for a month," said Joseph Morris. "And as the river is so near, they cannot very well close off our water supply."

"Jean Bevoir won't wait to starve us out," said Barringford. "He'll attack us, or do somethin' else, mark my words."

An early supper was had, and then the men on guard began a closer vigilance than ever. Every tree and bush and every rock without was closely watched. The tunnel had been shut up in such a way that it could not be used for the time being.

So far there had been little wind, but now a strong breeze came up. Hardly had it started than a shower of fire arrows came sailing over the stockade, to land in many directions.

"They are going to try to set fire to the buildings!" cried Dave.

"Put out the arrows!" cried Joseph Morris, and ran for some wet bags. With the bags the majority of the fire arrows were quickly extinguished. Two lodged on the roof of the main building, and Dave climbed up to put them out.

"Be careful,—don't expose yourself!" exclaimed his uncle.

The instant Dave made a whack with his wet bag at the fire arrow several other arrows flew in the direction, one striking his hunting shirt. The flame on it burnt fiercely and set fire to the youth's garments.

"Look out, you're burning!" cried one man.

"Roll down in the snow!" came from Sam Barringford.

This was good advice, and Dave lost no time in following it. Down he came in a pile of snow and rolled over and over, and the small blaze was immediately extinguished.

One of the arrows shot last had got a good hold between the logs of the roof and was burning at a lively rate.

"We ought to have some water," said Joseph Morris.

"Snow will do," answered the old frontiersman, and taking up a good-sized chunk, he hurled it at the arrow. His aim was good and the fire was blotted out. Then others took up handfuls of snow, and as soon as the burning arrows appeared, covered them completely; so that that new danger was quickly past.

The Indians under Moon Eye had hoped much from their burning arrows and were deeply chagrined to see them put out so easily. They sent out half a hundred or less and then ceased operations.

"The snow has aided them," grunted the chief in disgust. "We must try some other plan."

"Why not get a battering ram and ram down the gate?" asked Benoit Vascal of Jean Bevoir, in French.

The Frenchman suggested this to Moon Eye. The Indian leader was willing, provided the Frenchmen would use the ram, leaving the Indians to enter the post after the gate was down.

During the early part of the evening, another band of red men and several Frenchmen had come up, friendly to Moon Eye and to Bevoir. They joined forces with those besieging the post, making those without much stronger than before. Jean Bevoir promised the Indians and his countrymen all sorts of things if they would aid in capturing the post and in killing all the whites found defending it.

The plan to batter down the gate was carefully made. A fair-sized tree was cut down and trimmed off, leaving just enough of the branches to make good handles. This battering ram was brought up in the forest in a direct line with the stockade gate. At the front was placed a shield of loose branches and bark.

It the meantime, it was decided that six Indians should go to the rear of the post and make a demonstration there, shouting loudly and firing their guns and arrows,—doing this to draw the attention of the post defenders to that point. When the alarm was at its height, the battering ram was to be used with all force and as swiftly as possible. The moment the gate was down, Indians and Frenchmen were to rush into the post grounds and slaughter all who opposed them.

Having eaten his supper after the others, Sam Barringford walked around the entire stockade, questioning all who were on guard. Nobody had seen either a Frenchman or an Indian, although constantly on the alert.

"Tell ye wot I heard though," said one frontiersman to Barringford. "I heard 'em choppin' down a tree over yonder."

"Sure it war a tree, Collins?" asked the old frontiersman, with interest.

"I am."

"Humph!"

Sam Barringford said no more, but went straight to Joseph Morris.

"We want to watch thet gate harder nor ever," he announced.

"Why, Sam?"

"They have been cuttin' down a tree."

"Ha! Do you think they wish to use it for a battering ram?"

"Don't know wot else they'd want it fer. Anyway, it won't hurt to watch the gate extry well."

"I'll have it done," answered the planter, and was as good as his word.

Another hour went by and still the silence around the trading post continued. A few of the men were sleepy, but they were ordered to keep awake.

"Our sleeping will be done in the daytime after this—until the alarm is at an end," said Joseph Morris.

Suddenly there burst upon the night air a chorus of wild yells, coming from a point at the rear of the stockade. The six Indians sent to that place appeared, but took care to keep out of range of the frontiersmen's rifles.

"They are coming—over the back stockade!" was the cry.

"Don't run that way yet!" roared Sam Barringford. "Watch the gate! Watch the gate!"

Some of the men paused in bewilderment. Looking to the front, they could see nobody. From the rear a shot rang out, followed by several others, and then came a shower of arrows.

"Pretend to go back—and then turn and watch the gate," ordered Joseph Morris.

The men obeyed. But Dave remained at the gate, his eye glued to a near loophole. Only the stars were shining, so he had to watch closely in order to see anything at all.

The demonstration at the rear of the post went on, and now the Indians became a little bolder, running to within fifty yards of the palisade. As a consequence one received a bullet wound in his arm, and then all slipped behind the trees.

"Here they come!" yelled Dave, suddenly. "Here they come! Sam, quick! They have a battering ram!"

"Jest as I supposed!" returned the old frontiersman. "Give it to 'em, Dave!"

Crack! went the rifle of the youth and one of the Frenchmen carrying the ram staggered for a moment, grazed in the side. Then the crowd came forward, swiftly and silently. Barringford took aim and fired, and another Frenchman dropped back, seriously wounded. But the others did not pause.

Crash! The battering ram struck the gate with great force, causing it to quiver from top to bottom. But the posts and the oaken bars held, and those outside had to run back with the tree-trunk.

"Fire on 'em! Fire on 'em!" yelled Barringford, and he and Dave let drive a second time, and two other defenders followed suit. The men with the battering ram came up, but just as they were within three yards of the gate one of the leaders staggered and fell, shot through the knee. This confused the others, and the second blow on the gate was, consequently, a feeble one.

"Again! Again!" shrieked Jean Bevoir. "Up with the log!" he added, in French. "Remember the reward, if you get into the post! Now then, all together!"

Once more those outside raised the battering ram and ran back with it. They paused for a moment, to gather their strength. Then they hurled themselves forward, and the ram hit the gate with a crash that was deafening, causing the splinters to fly in all directions.

CHAPTER XXIX
FROM ENEMIES TO FRIENDS

It is now necessary to go back a little, to learn how poor Henry fared, after he and Sam Barringford escaped from the Indians who had made them prisoners.

Henry was on a good horse, but in leaping over some rocks the steed went down into a hollow, striking its head heavily. The youth was thrown off, and he and his steed were both stunned.

When Henry recovered he was again in the clutches of the red men. Three of them surrounded him and threatened to take his life on the spot if he did not submit, and they soon after bound his hands behind him with rawhides. The horse was found to be still fit for use, and Henry was bound on the animal's back. Then the party of Indians journeyed off to parts unknown.

Henry had suffered before, but now his red captors treated him worse than ever. They were a low grade of warriors, in reality outcasts, and hardly knew what to do with their white prisoner. They moved on for several miles, and then went into camp near the bank of the Ohio. Here they took Henry from the horse and fastened him to a tree. They had some food for themselves, but did not offer their captive a mouthful. They did, however, give him a drink, for which he was thankful.

Henry wondered if Barringford had escaped or been shot down. He saw no new scalp among the red men, which gave him a slight hope.

"If he got away maybe he will bring somebody to rescue me," thought the youth, but hour after hour went by, and nobody came near the camp.

Fortunately for Henry, the weather was exceedingly mild, so that he suffered little from the cold. He tried several times to question the Indians, but they understood little English and were not inclined to answer the questions he put. One slapped him in the face and another put a handful of soft snow down his back. Then they went away, to talk among themselves, leaving him alone.

He tried with might and main to either slip or break the bonds which bound him, but with no success. He looked around for some other means of getting away, but nothing presented itself.

Soon after consulting among themselves, some of the Indians went away, leaving only one red man on guard. This fellow, a warrior with a visage horribly pitted from smallpox, and a squint in one eye, wrapped himself in his blanket and sat down on a log, his bow and arrows across his knees.

A half-hour slipped by and the Indian dropped into a doze. Henry watched him with interest, and a little later saw that the warrior was fast asleep.

"Now, if only I could break these bonds and get away!" sighed the youth to himself.

Once again he went at the rawhide, but all he could do was to cut his wrists. At last he gave up in despair.

The other Indians came back soon after this, bringing some additional warriors with them. One could speak English, and he questioned Henry closely about himself and about those at the trading post.

"Let me go and I will reward you well," said Henry, after he saw that the red men had no intention of giving him his liberty.

Instead of agreeing to this, the Indian asked the youth about Jean Bevoir and Moon Eye. Then Henry was left once again to himself, while two Indians went off on a run,—to interview the French trader, as it afterwards proved.

The upshot of the matter was that Henry was taken to the camp Jean Bevoir and Moon Eye had made in the forest. Bevoir hailed the coming of the young prisoner with keen delight.

"Ha! so ve haf at least von of dem!" said he, rubbing his hands together. "How you like to be prisonair, hey?"

"Not at all," answered Henry, bluntly. "Now you have me, what do you intend to do, Jean Bevoir?"

"You shall soon see, *oui*! I haf not forgot ze past, no! no! I tak care of you, by gar!" And Jean Bevoir shook his fist in poor Henry's face.

"You will gain nothing by mistreating me," went on the youth, as steadily as he could. "Sooner or later the law will get hold of you. The best thing you can do is to let me go."

"I not let you go. Ve shall fight zem at ze post. Ve vin sure—but if ve lose, hey? I haf you, hey? Vat can za do to Jean Bevoir if you be a prisonair, hey? If za keel me den my men keel you! Now you understand, *oui*?"

Henry did understand, and it made his heart sink lower than ever. By holding him a prisoner the Frenchman expected to keep himself from harm. If he was captured he would warn his captors not to harm him, otherwise Henry must suffer.

The preparations for attacking the post were now going forward, and a little later Henry was removed in the care of two Indians to a station still further up the Ohio. Here some of the red men had something of a village, and here, to his astonishment, the youth found many of the horses of the pack-train and also the sick man who had so mysteriously disappeared.

The sick man lay in a wigwam on some blankets. Strange to relate, his recent adventures had not made him any weaker than he had formerly been; in fact, they appeared to have helped him.

"I, too, tried to get away, on one of the horses," he said. "But some Indians followed me up, and captured me. They brought me to this place, and an old Indian medicine man gave me some medicine which has helped me wonderfully."

The man then wanted to know something about Henry, and the youth told him as much as he deemed necessary. The two were in the midst of the conversation when two Indians came in and hustled Henry out of the wigwam and to another part of the village.

"White people talk too much," said one of the Indians, thereby giving the youth to understand that they did not wish the pair to consult together.

From what little Henry had learned he was now certain that a strong attack was to be made on the trading post. As a consequence he wanted to get free more than ever, that he might warn his friends.

His bonds were not the same as those which had kept him a prisoner before, and by working diligently over them, he managed at last to get one hand free. The other quickly followed, and then he freed his feet.

He was alone in the wigwam, the Indians in the village having gathered to hold a pow-wow, the question being how much they should do to aid Moon Eye and Jean Bevoir. The Indians had no desire to become hurt in a battle, yet they were anxious to obtain some of the many gifts which Bevoir had promised them in case of a victory over the English.

With great caution Henry looked out of the wigwam and surveyed the situation. The camp was close to the river bank and was backed up by the virgin forest, which, at this point, was rough and uncertain. It would be an easy matter to hide in the forest, but the question arose, what should he do when he got there?

"Well, anything is better than being a prisoner," he mused. "I'll take what I can lay my hands on and get out."

He looked about him and managed to secure an old hunting knife and likewise a pretty fair bow and several arrows. It was growing dark, and at the risk of being seen he stole to a place where the Indians had stored some blankets and some provisions. He supplied himself with what he wanted, and then, like a ghost, glided into the mighty forest.

"Now for the trading post," he muttered to himself. "By hook or crook, I must get there, and pray Heaven I get there before it is too late!"

He knew that in order to reach the post he would have to keep close to the river. He imagined the trading post was about three miles away, although he was by no means sure.

Traveling through the forest in the dark proved to be a harder task than Henry had anticipated. He went plunging along until several falls knocked the wind completely out of him and barked his shins mightily. At last he had to give it up and turned to the river, resolved to travel on the ice, even though the danger might be greater.

Coming down to the open he gazed around, and seeing nobody, stepped on the ice. It appeared to be firm, and he started on a swift trot, straight for the trading post.

Crack! Henry had not been on the ice over a minute when this ominous sound greeted him. He had come to where the surface was more than slushy. The ice bent beneath him.

"This won't do!" he cried, and tried to turn toward the shore once more. But the movement came too late; down went the ice and Henry with it, and the next instant he was over his head in the chilling water.

Had Henry not been so robust and such a good swimmer he would have perished on the spot. As it was, the coldness of the water almost paralyzed him, and when he went down he could do little but gasp and splutter and reach out blindly. Then, when he came up, his head hit the under surface of the ice, and down he went as before.

The sturdy youth now realized that he had a life or death struggle before him. No one was at hand to give him aid, and if he was to be saved he must do it himself. As he came up once more he clutched at the under surface of the ice and felt around until he found something of an opening. Then, with might and main, he pulled himself up, until his head and shoulders were out of the water. It was high time, for he could no longer hold his breath.

The ice was all around him, but so rotten that it threatened at every instant to break away and let him down again. He was less than ten yards from the bank of the river, but try his best he could make no headway toward safety.

As Henry was wondering how long he could stand the cold and keep from losing his grip something along the shore attracted his attention. He gave a closer look and saw three Indians stealing along. That they were enemies he had not the slightest doubt, yet he hailed their appearance with a certain sense of joy. They could save him, even though they might make him their prisoner once more.

"Help!" he called, as loudly as he could. "Help!"

The Indians were at first startled by the call, and in a trice fled behind some trees and out of sight. But then they saw the youth's head and noted his plight and came forth and ran to the edge of the river bank.

"Help me!" went on Henry. "Do not let me drown!"

"We help," grunted one of the Indians, and threw out a lasso he chanced to be carrying. It fell within Henry's reach, and he quickly grasped it. Then the three red men hauled him to a place of safety.

"My friend Henry!" cried one of the red men, in amazement.

"White Buffalo!" gasped the youth. "Can it be possible? How came you here?"

"White Buffalo is journeying to the trading post. He heard that harm had befallen his old friends," answered the old chief of the Delawares. "Is his friend Henry alone?"

"Yes. I was out with Sam Barringford, and we were captured by some unfriendly Indians," returned Henry, and related his story in detail, to which White Buffalo listened with close attention. Then the chief asked about Joseph Morris, Dave, and also about Jean Bevoir and Moon Eye.

"Bevoir and Moon Eye are snakes, not fit to live," said White Buffalo. "A runner brought me the news of what was being done. If they have slain my friend James Morris both of them shall die. White Buffalo swears it by the Great Spirit."

"Have you only these two warriors with you?"

"No, close at hand White Buffalo has two score men—the flower of his warriors. Our tribe is united and in the future all will fight only for the English. We shall aid in driving the French and the bad Indians from the land."

"Good for you!" cried Henry. The news made his heart give a bound. "If you intend to help us, the quicker you get to the trading post the better."

"It shall be as my brother Henry wills," answered the chief. "But Henry cannot travel while he is wet and cold. Here, let him take White Buffalo's blanket," and the chief passed it over.

"Thank you, the blanket and walking will keep me warm. Let us get your men together without delay and start for the post. For all I know the attack may have already begun!"

They left the vicinity of the Ohio and plunged straight into the forest. While hurrying along White Buffalo explained that he had been out scouting, to note how matters were going. In their march westward they had encountered several wandering Indians who had told them of some of the doings of Jean Bevoir and Moon Eye.

"I cannot believe that my friend and brother, James Morris, is dead," said the old chief, sadly. "It is hard upon my young friend Dave."

"That it is," answered Henry. "I am afraid Dave won't care for the post any more, even if it is saved."

As soon as they came to the Indians' stopping-place White Buffalo delivered a brief address to his braves. They were perfectly willing to do whatever he wanted of them; and in a few minutes the whole party set off for the trading post.

CHAPTER XXX
FOR LIFE OR DEATH

"The gate is giving way!" cried one of the frontiersmen, when the battering ram had struck it once more with tremendous force.

"This way, everybody!" called out Joseph Morris. "We must fight for it now!"

Half a dozen were already stationed at convenient loopholes and were pouring in a constant fire on the Frenchmen. Several went down, but the others kept at the work. Jean Bevoir had furnished them with all they wished of strong liquor, and many were reckless to the last degree.

On the edge of the forest Moon Eye waited with the majority of the savage warriors under him. He saw the gate quiver and splinter, and then, as there came another onslaught, ordered his braves to advance. On they came, yelling like demons, and sending a flight of arrows over the stockade.

Sam Barringford was in his element, and from a loophole nearest to the gate he continued to shoot at the Frenchmen. But some of the attackers had stuck slabs of wood into their girdles in front, and these slabs acted as shields.

"They are coming again!" cried Dave. He stood with his eye to a loophole, his gun smoking from a recent discharge. "They are bound to get in."

"Look at the Indians!" shrieked one of the frontiersmen. "They have been reinforced! There must be half a hundred of them!"

"If they come in, perhaps we had better retreat to the main building," suggested Joseph Morris. "We cannot stand up against more than twice our own number."

The Indians who had been making the demonstration in the rear of the trading post, now came around to the front. At the same time the Frenchmen prepared for a last attack on the gate. On they came with a force that nothing could resist. Crash! came the battering ram and snap! crash! went the gate, the oaken bars splitting and breaking and sending a shower of splinters over those behind. Then the gate went down in the snow and mud.

"'Tis down! 'Tis down!" Frenchmen and Indians gave a cheer and a yell. Those who had been handling the battering ram stepped to one side, and on swept the warriors under Moon Eye, straight for the opening that had been created in the stockade.

"Hold 'em back!" yelled Sam Barringford, stepping to the center of the gateway. "Give it to 'em hot! Don't let a skunk o' 'em git in!" And he blazed away at one of the leading Indians. The warrior pitched headlong and the man behind went down on top of him.

Dave, his uncle, and many of the others, also fired, and four of the red warriors were either killed or mortally wounded. There was a brief pause, and then Moon Eye urged his braves to go on.

"Yes! yes!" yelled Jean Bevoir. "At zem! At zem! Keel zem all! A big, big reward shall be yours if ve capture ze post!"

"Go to the front—do some fighting yourself!" growled Benoit Vascal. He had received an ugly wound in the forearm.

"I am not afraid," answered Jean Bevoir, recklessly. He too had been drinking freely. And forward he rushed, and some of his countrymen with him, following up the Indians to the gateway of the stockade.

The battle was now on in all its fury. Two of the frontiersmen had been shot down and Sam Barringford had been struck in the thigh. Dave was on the point of using the pistol he carried when a warrior hit him in the side with an arrow.

"Dave!" cried Joseph Morris, in alarm, but could say no more, for he found himself confronted also, and had to fight his best to save his life. He was struck by a bullet in the shoulder, but the wound was of small consequence.

The noise was now terrific, the Indians yelling like demons and the guns and pistols being discharged freely. Some of the contestants were at it hand-to-hand, with hunting knives, tomahawks, and clubs. Slowly but surely the English were driven back from the gateway, and Indians and French began to crowd into the trading post enclosure.

"We can't keep this up! They are too many for us!" gasped one of the frontiersmen. The blood was pouring from a cut in his cheek. "It's three or four to one!"

"It's for life or death!" came from another. "Don't give in! The Indians will show no mercy! We must fight to a finish!"

All realized the truth of the speaker's remarks. The Indians would surely kill them all or else make them prisoners first and torture them to death afterwards. It would be better to die fighting than to allow themselves to be captured.

In the midst of the noise and excitement a yell was heard from the forest, and then followed several scattering shots. No one paid attention to these for the minute, but soon came a yell that caused the Indians under Moon Eye to listen in consternation. It was the war-cry of the Delawares, and it told that they were about to enter the fray.

"What's that?" came from Joseph Morris.

"I know what it is!" yelled Dave. His heart gave a bound. "That is White Buffalo's war-whoop!"

"White Buffalo is comin'!" came from Sam Barringford. He gave an answering cry at the top of his lungs. "I only hope he has a good followin'! We need 'em!"

The band under White Buffalo was coming forward on a run, firing rapidly. With the aged chief was Henry, who had cast aside the blanket, forgetting in his excitement that he was soaked from his involuntary bath in the river.

"Give it to 'em!" shouted Henry, firing a gun that had been given to him. "Shoot 'em down! They deserve it! And don't let any of the Frenchmen get away!"

The Delawares came up directly behind Moon Eye's band, and their first volley of shots and arrows laid four of the enemy low. Then they fired once more and closed in with hunting knives and hatchets, doing fearful execution. In the midst of the slaughter was White Buffalo, his teeth set, his eyes flashing, and his whole demeanor the personification of courage and daring. Of all the whites he had ever known, the Morrises were his dearest friends, and he was more than ready to lay down his life for them.

The coming of White Buffalo with his band gave fresh courage to Joseph Morris and those under him, and they renewed with vigor the fight they were making in the trading post yard. In the meantime the Indians under Moon Eye and the Frenchmen scarcely knew what to do.

"The Delawares have come to give us battle!" cried one of Moon Eye's under chiefs.

"They are strong and fresh!" added another, who was sorely wounded in the leg.

"We are hemmed in!" came from one of the Frenchmen. "Reinforcements for the post have arrived!"

Loud yells and more shots drowned out the words spoken after that. The din became louder than ever and the smoke rolled upward from every direction. Henry was in a fierce hand-to-hand fight with one of the Indians when Benoit Vascal limped past.

"Ha! It ees you!" shrieked the Frenchman, and made a lunge at Henry with his hunting knife. But at that moment White Buffalo threw his tomahawk at Vascal. The rascal received a glancing blow that stretched him senseless. Then over his body rushed some Indians, and he was, for the time being, forgotten.

The coming of the Delawares was disconcerting to Jean Bevoir. It came at a moment when he had felt certain victory would soon rest with himself and Moon Eye. He and his followers were practically caught, some inside of the gateway and some outside, and knew not how to turn. A galling fire was poured into them by the newcomers, and fully a dozen Indians and Frenchmen went down never to rise again. Bevoir was hit in the shoulder and later received a knife stab in the side.

For fully ten minutes the battle continued, but then, as he saw his warriors being slaughtered, Moon Eye lost heart, and sounded the retreat. The Indians under him got out of the gateway as best they could and scattered to the right and left, some running along the river and others taking to the shelter of the forest.

"After them!" said White Buffalo, to his braves, in his native tongue. "Let not one of them escape. They are vile creatures, not fit to live, enemies of us all!" And away went his braves after the others, following Moon Eye's men for over a mile and killing fully half of them. Moon Eye himself was struck by a bullet in the back and fell, and a few minutes later White Buffalo finished the rascal with his tomahawk.

As soon as they saw that their Indian allies were retreating, the Frenchmen also tried to retire. All told they now numbered five, including Jean Bevoir. They sneaked along the stockade until they came to a point nearest to the mighty forest and then made a break for the trees. Those at the post fired several shots after them, but these did no harm.

"Where is Jean Bevoir?" asked Joseph Morris, as the battle came to an end.

"He got away," answered Barringford, who was panting from his exertions. "Drat the luck! He'll come back, I reckon, to make more trouble for us some other time."

"Dave, you are wounded," said his uncle.

"It doesn't matter," answered the youth, bravely. "Oh, how glad I am that White Buffalo came up! We should have lost had it not been for him and his warriors."

"He has gone after what's left of the other redskins," said one of the frontiersmen. "I hope he kills them all!"

Joseph Morris and Dave were overjoyed to see Henry back again and gave the youth a warm greeting. Torches were lit, and a list made of the dead and wounded, and the latter were made as comfortable as possible.

"I vote to go after Jean Bevoir," said Dave. "I must catch that man and make him tell me all he knows about father."

"An' I am with ye, lad," said Barringford. "It ain't right to let thet hound git away. He has caused all o' us trouble enough."

"We cannot go away and leave the post alone," said Joseph Morris. "Bevoir might come back in the meantime and take possession."

"We can fool him," said Dave. "Let us raise the gate and fasten it in some manner and then leave a few men on guard. He won't know but what all of us are inside."

This was considered a good plan, and leaving the dead where they had fallen, those able to work quickly set the broken gate into place and propped it fast with some heavy logs. Then seven of the party, including the planter, Barringford, Dave, and Henry, left the post and took to the forest in the direction Jean Bevoir and his followers had gone.

"Be careful," warned Sam Barringford. "We don't want to run into a trap. Remember, Jean Bevoir is foxy, an' always was."

The night was still fairly clear, and they followed the trail through the wet snow with ease. Evidently the Frenchman had not imagined that he would be pursued, and so had not taken any precautions to hide his tracks. The trail led straight forward for nearly a mile, then curved in the direction of the river.

"I believe he is bound for that Indian village I was at," said Henry, who had, during the brief rest at the post, donned some dry clothing. "Perhaps he hopes to get aid there. Well, he will be disappointed, I think, although I am not sure."

As they drew closer to the village they advanced with increased caution, and each member of the party looked to make sure that his weapons were in proper order. All were tired out, and each was more or less wounded, but none thought of giving up the task they had undertaken.

Dave was particularly eager to meet Bevoir and, if possible, make the rascally French trader a prisoner. He felt that Bevoir was the only one to give him all the particulars of his father's death and burial, and he felt that if the Frenchman got away now he might remain away forever.

At last they saw a distant gleam of light through the forest and knew that the Indian camp was not far off. They moved ahead slower than ever.

"I see somebody moving around!" cried Dave, in a low voice. "I think it is an Indian."

"I see two Indians," said Sam Barringford. "But they are old men and unarmed."

They drew closer still, until only a fringe of bushes hid the dark camp from view. The campfire had burned low, and they could see that the most of the wigwams had been taken down. Evidently what was left of the tribe were getting ready to leave that vicinity.

Presently they heard sounds from the opposite side of the camp, and two Indians and three Frenchmen appeared, leading a number of horses.

"There is Jean Bevoir now," whispered Henry.

"Yes, and those horses are our own," answered his father.

The horses were stopped at the doorway of one of the wigwams and an Indian went in, to appear a moment later leading the sick man whom Henry had seen but a few hours before.

"Where are you going to take me?" asked the man, feebly.

"You vill know zat in ze morning," answered Jean Bevoir. "You shall ride a horse."

Then Bevoir entered another wigwam. Soon he came forth, dragging another man by the arm.

"Don't!" gasped the man, feebly. "Don't! I—I cannot stand it! Have a little mercy, Bevoir, I—I beg of you!" And the man fell in a heap.

"Git up!" roared Jean Bevoir, savagely. "You shall come with me. Dead or alive, I shall take you avay!"

"See! see!" shrieked Dave, forgetting himself completely. "See, it is my father! Jean Bevoir, let him alone, or I'll shoot you on the spot!"

CHAPTER XXXI
DAYS OF PEACE—CONCLUSION

It was indeed James Morris who lay on the ground at Jean Bevoir's feet.

The trader had not been killed, only seriously wounded, and for days had lain between life and death, in the care of an old Indian medicine man. Many a time the French trader had thought to slay him, but had hesitated, thinking he might some day make use of his prisoner.

James Morris was still so weak that he could do nothing for himself, yet Jean Bevoir wanted him to mount a horse and ride away, to a cave up the river, where, in years gone by, the French trader and his trappers had had a regular rendezvous.

It made Dave's blood boil to see his father so abused, and forgetful of everything else, he ran forward, leveling his rifle at Bevoir's head as he did so.

"Dave! My son Dave!" cried James Morris, and there was a ring of relief and joy in his tones.

"Father!" was all the son answered. He still kept his eyes on the French trader, who shrank back in consternation.

"Come on, all of you!" cried Joseph Morris, who now saw that further secrecy would be useless. "Surrender, you villains, or we'll shoot you down like dogs!"

"Thet's the talk!" came from Barringford, and as he saw one of the Indians raise a gun he shot the warrior through the heart.

The next instant the entire camp was in alarm. Thinking a large body of English had arrived, the few Indians present took to their heels and disappeared into the forest as if by magic. The Frenchmen tried to follow, fighting as they did so. Jean Bevoir aimed a pistol at Dave and fired, the bullet striking the youth in the side. As he staggered and fell Henry fired at the French trader, and so did two others, and Bevoir threw up his arms and pitched headlong into the smoldering campfire, scattering the embers in all directions.

Inside of five minutes the battle was at an end and the English were in complete possession of the camp and had also gained possession of their horses and a large portion of their stores. What was left of the French and Indians disappeared, and that was the last seen of them.

Bevoir pitched headlong into the smoldering campfire.

Dave's wound was but slight, and his first thoughts were of his father. The two embraced over and over again, the tears of joy standing in the eyes of each. Joseph Morris, Henry, and Barringford were likewise more than happy to learn that the trader was really alive.

"I am the only one living to tell the tale," said James Morris. "The others were killed or mortally wounded."

"Not all," answered Dave. "Peaceful Jones escaped and told us the news, and that is what brought us here so quickly."

"You have had a great fight. I could hear some of the shooting," continued the trader.

"Yes, and we might have had the worst of it, only White Buffalo came to our aid."

"And where is he now?"

"Gone in pursuit of Moon Eye and his followers."

After that James Morris told his story in detail, to which Dave and the others listened with much interest.

"At first I was kept at the post," said he. "Jean Bevoir pretended to be kind and considerate, but I soon found out his object. He had drawn up some documents stating that I surrendered to him all my rights and interests in the trading post and he wanted me to sign them. When I refused he got angry and wanted to kill me. But some of the men interfered and then I was brought to this place. Then, of a sudden, I was treated better again. From the Indians I learned that Bevoir had an idea that if he got cornered later on he would use me in some way for his benefit—as a hostage, or something like that."

"Just what he wanted to do with me, when I was a prisoner," said Henry. "It is queer that I didn't see you when I was here," he added.

"They must have kept us apart purposely, Henry." James Morris drew a long breath. "How good it feels to be together once more. I declare, it seems to brace me up wonderfully!" And his face showed his relief.

Somebody had dragged Jean Bevoir's body from the fire just after the man fell. The trader was not yet dead, and lay groaning and writhing in a fearful manner. Nothing could be done for him, and he died at sunrise. It was the last of a misspent life, full of golden opportunities which the rascal had trampled under foot. His body was laid in a hollow and some flat stones placed over it, to keep off the wild animals. His pockets were searched and the fraudulent documents confiscated by Joseph Morris.

"We must get back to the post as soon as we can," said Barringford, after the excitement was over. "Remember, we don't know how matters are a-goin' there."

"I have heard no shots," answered Henry. "And that is a good sign."

"I do not see how anything can be wrong there," said Dave. "We have wound up the Bevoir crowd and you can trust White Buffalo to take care of Moon Eye's tribe."

Nevertheless, the start for the trading post was made as soon as matters could be gotten into shape for the journey. The two sick men were carried on stretchers made of blankets tied to long poles, and all took turns at the task. Dave did not mind the load at all, and in the joy at finding his parent forgot all about his own injuries, which, fortunately, proved slight.

The strange man who was sick wanted to know what it all meant, and smiled when told. Then he heaved a sudden sigh.

"I, too, have had many troubles," he said. "Many, many troubles. I wish that I could get some help."

"We will aid you all we can," said Henry, kindly.

"Yes, yes, I know. But my head—it is not clear. My brain whirls when I try to think. The past is such a blank!"

"You were hit on the head, that's the trouble," went on the youth. "But I think you will get over it soon."

"Perhaps—some days I know I feel better. But then my head whirls again and I am in the dark! Oh, it is awful!" And the sick man sighed as before.

"Can't you remember where you came from at all?"

"I remember the sea—the great boundless ocean, and a great storm. I was alone then—all alone. And I remember before that,—a beautiful garden and kind friends and relatives, and the babies, the beautiful babies! And then I remember—I remember——" The man paused. "It is cloudy again—dark—I can remember nothing, nothing!" And he lay back and closed his eyes.

"Maybe as how he'll never be jest right ag'in," whispered Sam Barringford. "It's terribul, no two ways on't! I wish I could do somethin' fer him."

"It will take time," said Joseph Morris. "It is useless to worry him now, it will only make matters worse." And so they let the strange man rest in peace. They had previously searched his pockets, but had found nothing by which he could be identified.

The journey to the trading post accomplished, they found matters quiet there. No more of the enemy had appeared, and nothing had been seen of White Buffalo and his followers. The old Delaware chief came in about noon, bringing the news that Moon Eye's tribe had been completely shattered.

"They will never trouble my white friends again," said White Buffalo. "Those who are left alive have learned a lesson which they will never forget."

The old Indian chief was more than glad to learn that James Morris was living, and shook hands warmly.

"You have done me and mine a great service, White Buffalo," said the trader, gratefully. "We shall not forget it."

"White Buffalo knows his real friends," answered the aged chief, calmly. "He is glad to serve them." Then he and his warriors went off to get something to eat, for they had had nothing since the day before. They were treated to the best the post afforded.

Among those found living after the battle at the post was Benoit Vascal. He had been sorely wounded and trampled upon in the mêlée, and it was evident he could not long survive his hurts. He was placed on a rude couch and there he remained, since he could swallow neither food nor water. He groaned continually and bitterly bewailed the fate that had brought him to the place.

When the strange sick man was brought in he was placed on a cot not far from where Benoit Vascal was resting. For some time the two did not notice each other. Then, of a sudden, the Frenchman glanced at the other and uttered a shriek of amazement and terror.

"'Tis he! 'Tis he! 'Tis the judgment!" he screamed in French. "Take him away! I cannot bear to face him!"

At the sound of Vascal's voice the strange sick man turned over and gave him a wandering look. Then he also started up and gave a cry.

"You! you!" he screamed. "You! I know you, Benoit Vascal! What have you done with my children!" He staggered from his couch, fell forward, and caught the Frenchman by the arm. "Tell me! My children, what of them?"

"What's the matter here?" demanded Sam Barringford, who chanced to be close by.

"This man!" panted the strange sick man. "He—he stole my children! He is the rascal I have been hunting for—he and another, a Paul Camont. They took my twin boys! Ah, I remember it all now! Where are my children? Don't dare to say you killed them!"

"Your children—twins," gasped the old frontiersman. "Can it be possible thet you air Mr. Maurice Hamilton?"

"Yes! yes! that is my name! How strange I could not think of it before. Maurice Hamilton, yes, of London."

"Well, by the eternal!" came faintly from Barringford. He looked at the sick man sharply. "It must be so—ye look alike, same eyes, same nose, an' all. This staggers me!"

"Let me go!" came faintly from Benoit Vascal. "He has ze children—I haf zem not, no! Let me go!" for the other man now held him by the throat.

The cries and loud talking had attracted a crowd, and all pushed forward to learn the cause of the disturbance.

"It's the greatest thing ye ever heard tell on," said Sam Barringford. "This man is Maurice Hamilton, and the father o' the twins."

"Can it be possible!" exclaimed Dave.

"But where—where are my children?" asked Maurice Hamilton.

"They are safe—leas'wise they war, the last I heard o' 'em," answered Barringford. "But this gits me! I never dreamed o' sech a thing."

"Nor did I," added Joseph Morris.

After that there remained nothing to do but to tell Maurice Hamilton all about his little ones, how Barringford had found them, and how they had been cared for ever since by the Morrises. The sick man could not take it all in, but he understood enough and the tears of joy streamed down his wan face.

"How I long to see them—my darling boys!" he murmured.

"And you shall see them," said Joseph Morris. "But first you must get well."

"And what of—of that rascal who robbed me?"

"He is dying—let him rest," was the planter's soft answer. And then, for the time being, Maurice Hamilton was silent. From that hour on he mended rapidly, both mentally and physically, until, two months later, he was as well as ever. Benoit Vascal died two days later, and was buried in a common grave, along with the other Frenchmen who had fallen in the battle for the possession of the trading post.

Maurice Hamilton's story was a long one, and I have no space to relate it here. He was a fairly well-to-do man who, after the death of his beautiful wife and his father and mother, had come to America to seek his fortune. Upon arriving here his twins had been stolen from him by Benoit Vascal, aided by Paul Camont. He had in vain tried to follow the rascals up, although he had received several letters offering to compromise the matter for a certain amount. He said that his wife, when a girl, had received an offer of marriage from Vascal and had refused him, and this had made the Frenchman so bitter. The two gold lockets the twins possessed contained the portraits of Mr. Hamilton's father and mother.

"This clears up that mystery," said Dave to Henry. "I must say I am glad of it—on Mr. Hamilton's account."

"Yes, and also on account of the twins," answered his cousin. "But Sam will hate to have them go, and mother and Nell will hate it, too."

"Well, such things can't be helped."

Now that the fighting was over, all hands found a great many things to do in and around the trading post. A new gate was put into place, stronger even than the other, and the stockade generally was also strengthened. The stable was enlarged, so that the numerous horses might have proper quarters, and another room was built to the main building. In the meantime some of the trappers and Indians went out on the hunt and brought in plenty of meat and not a few skins of value.

With the coming of spring came a fresh alarm, and it was not deemed wise to send an expedition eastward. Pontiac was trying his best to combine the Indians in another conspiracy. But his plans failed, and in the end the noted Indian chief fell, brained by a tomahawk in the hands of another Indian. So perished one of the most gifted and at the same time one of the most warlike Indian chiefs this country ever saw.

At last the way seemed clear for a start for Will's Creek, and an expedition set out, by way of Fort Pitt. Among those to go along were Joseph Morris, Sam Barringford, Mr. Hamilton, and Henry. Mr. Hamilton was feeling in the best of health once more, and he and the old frontiersman had become warm friends. The gentleman wanted to reward Barringford for what he had done, but the latter would not listen to it.

"Let me see them twins now an' then," said the old frontiersman. "Thet will be reward enough fer me." And so it was arranged.

It was a great day when the party reached the Morris homestead. Maurice Hamilton hugged his children tightly to his breast and kissed them repeatedly, and Mrs. Morris was so affected that she wept.

"They are good boys," she said. "I'll hate awfully to have them go away."

"Then supposing I leave them here for the present?" answered Maurice Hamilton. "I have no home of my own."

"Yes! yes! Do leave them, please!" cried Nell; and so it was arranged, much to the satisfaction of all concerned.

Here let me add a few words and then bring to a close this story of "Trail and Trading Post," and likewise this "Colonial Series."

During the ensuing summer matters fared very well both at the Morris homestead and at the trading post. The twins grew up healthy and strong, and looked upon Sam Barringford as their uncle, which pleased the old frontiersman mightily. Mr. Hamilton came and went, for he had property on the St. Lawrence and near Philadelphia to look after. He was glad to have his children in such excellent care.

"I hope them little chaps never see sech fightin' as we've seen," said Barringford to Henry one day, as he was dancing both on his knees.

"I don't think they will," answered Henry. But he was mistaken. The twins did see some spirited fighting—during the Revolutionary War—the particulars of which I may relate some other time. They were such sturdy, manly chaps that nobody could help but like them.

During the summer the trading post was attacked just once, by a band of Indians, under an old chief who in years gone by had been one of the Morrises' worst foes. The warriors were defeated without a loss among the whites, while the Indians lost several men, including the chief. After that the red men remained away from that territory for many years to come.

As soon as peace was firmly established, other traders flocked to the Ohio, followed by regular settlers. Many of the posts were valuable, but none more so than that belonging to the Morrises. More than this, James Morris and Dave dealt fairly by all who wished to do business with them, be they whites or Indians, and as a consequence they soon established a reputation that was known far and wide. The very best skins and furs were offered to them, and they began to make money rapidly.

"How things have changed since first we came out here," said Dave one day. "And what a number of events have happened since then!"

"Let us be thankful that all has ended well," replied his father. "Many have suffered deeply, while we have escaped."

"I am thankful," said Dave, reverently. "Very thankful indeed!"

White Buffalo, who stood near, nodded his head slowly.

"The Great Spirit has watched over us all," said he. "Blessed be the Great Spirit, both of the white man and of the Indians."

THE END